HELP, HELP AMERICA

LEADERSHIP, ROLES, AND RESPONSIBILITY

DR. FRANCIS S. LAARI

HELP AMERICA

Leadership, Roles, and Responsibilities

Dr. Francis Songtiib. Laari

Kravitz & Sons
INNOVATORS IN PUBLISHING, MARKETING AND ADVERTISING

Kravitz and Sons LLC
1301 Farmville Blvd, Suite 104
Greenville, NC 27834

Published by Kravitz and Sons LLC.

ISBN: 979-8-89639-348-1 (sc)
ISBN: 979-8-89639-347-4 (e)

Library of Congress Control Number: ___________

It takes only one person.

The World Trade Center is gone. The January 6 insurrection rioted in Capitol Hill, while the COVID-19 pandemic was undermined by leadership. The US government withdrew from Afghanistan, the US southern borders flooded with immigrants, Goerge Floyd was killed, and people were kneeling while the national anthem was sung. Confederate monuments were taken down, and the US gun rights were attacked while mental health awareness in the country was undermined.

However, it takes only one person to make a difference in leadership, roles, and responsibility. Leadership does not go around issues, rather they are supposed to confront them. This is what President W. Bush did during the 9/11 attack. He confronted the enemy right from ground zero. He flew from Washington and landed right in the middle of ground zero in New York City with his microphone and spoke to all Americans.

"I hear you!"

It is how leadership takes its leadership roles and responsibility to the highest level of government. It is how leadership becomes clear in society. Because the legacy is prominent for the young youth to learn and carry over to the next generation of leadership. However, such leadership is diminishing in American society. Because people are undermining the power of the oath and constitution and want to remain as followers rather than pursuing leadership roles and responsibilities that they are destined to do.

Denying political floods.

While the United States of America is known for its oath and constitution, the country is struggling with leadership, role, and responsibility issues. Nobody cares about the oath and constitution anymore, but politics and the political party. Whatever actions, Regardless of how politics are affecting every level of government, citizens, the community, and the wellbeing of the nation, everybody is in denial. It is a political flood. It is wiping the values of the country away from the people. There is no balance between the law and society. All decisions across the country are based on the values of Democrats or Republicans. What about the independents?

Nobody cares about the nation's youth any longer or the future of the country. It is a political flood. Once you are supporting my party, you are covered. Don't worry about your flip-flops. There are no such guiding principles in the party membership and leadership to worry about. There is no system in place to intervene in any political flood in a party or nation. There is no independent voice institution that is not bonded by Democrats or Republicans and has a leadership role and responsibility to reflect on issues that matter the most for the country. Due to this, there are increasing political floods flooding over the nation, which in turn, impact the leadership and political infrastructure of the country.

Leadership and party affiliation.

Due to political appointments and Party affiliations, many leaders have undermined their leadership. They do not want to pursue justice and positive change. They feel obligated to cover issues rather than to correct them. They want to stay within the boundaries of the political party rather than standing up for the values of the country, leadership, roles, and responsibility. As a result, the vision that our ancestors had for this country is left behind.

Due to these political floods, potential leaders of the country are left in the hood. They will never speak out. Instead, they will try to adapt themselves to the personality that does not fit them to fit into the political party. They pass on their leadership to others. Due to this, many politicians have no business in their leadership, role, and responsibility but in politics. These political floods are gradually clouding the entire leadership of the nation. This pattern of political floods does not help leadership assume its leadership role and responsibility and pursue fairness. Eventually, these clouds are going to cover the traditional values of the nation's leadership at home and abroad and create political tension between the country and its allies.

Broken legislative bonds in Congress.

Within the past decade, Congress has changed the leadership and political culture of the United States. The Congressmen and women are not cohesively working together. Unfortunately, they have taken political issues personally. Many leaders have personalized their leadership, role, and responsibility to the country to suit their political needs or personal self by clinging to a political party rather than the country. I would think that everybody would think about the country first before the political party. But this is the opposite. People are thinking about the political party more than the country. This is where the divisiveness of the Congress is coming from because Congress is a two-way street: Democrats or Republicans.

There are not any other party members to balance the weaknesses and leaderships of both parties. Until this happens, America's political system will lack surveillance on the blank spots of leadership, role, and responsibility. Today, many politicians think that leadership can do anything without a role and responsibility or legal consequences. If your party has the majority in Congress, you can do whatever you want, they will cover you up. How long will Congress continue to cover people who do not want to assume their leadership roles and responsibility for the country? This is a political flood. It affects not only the youth who are learning and integrating into the political culture of the country but also the integrity of the nation.

Leadership, role, and responsibility

It is now impossible not to call you and everybody across the country individually or collectively to help, help the United States of America. This is a call to draw the attention of the entire nation to the new definition of leadership, role, and responsibility. How do you lead people if you do not understand your leadership? How do you affect your leadership if you do not understand your role? How can you account for your leadership if you do not understand your responsibility?

Regardless of your level of leadership, if you do not understand your leadership role and responsibility, you are going to create a political flood in the environment of your leadership. It will not only affect the people that you work with, but also it will affect the people that you serve. It is critical to learn and know your leadership, roles, and responsibilities. It is not political.

The root cause of weaknesses in leadership.

What you think is political or politics could be a weakness in leadership roles and responsibility. Since the death of George Floyd, the January 6 insurrection, withdrawal from Afghanistan, the US southern border immigration crisis, and government shutdown initiatives in Congress, everybody is wiping off leadership, role, and responsibility arguing that these actions are insignificant. All supporters, Democrats or Republicans are cheering on and chanting in them move-on, move-on, suggesting that George Floyd's death, the January 6 insurrection, withdrawal from Afghanistan, and the US Southern Borders' immigration issues, and the government shutdown initiatives are just realities to deal with, it has no negative impact on the youth and future leadership, role, and responsibility in the country.

As time passed, people became comfortable with the concerns of George Floyd's death, the January 6 insurrection, withdrawal from Afghanistan, the immigration issues at the US Southern Borders, and the government shutdown initiatives. With politicians, it is a new culture of politics, it has no legal ramifications to worry about it. While these are politically fair in the United States, they lack theoretical features to address positive social change. It has no social change implication in leadership, role, and responsibility.

A change that the youth and future leaders can replicate. Is there anybody who is not called for a duty? Once you have life, you have duty. If you are called for a duty, you have a leadership role and responsibility for the duty. Everybody has a leadership role and responsibility because everybody is destined for a duty from the day they were born until then whether you are a child, parent, educator, or politician. This is how leadership is defined. Leadership is not like a manager in the grocery store, governor of the state, or the president of the United States, but you. You have a leadership role and responsibility as a child, parent, educator, governor, or the president of the United States for your actions.

Leadership disarmed their leadership.

Regardless of these critical matters that affect the leadership of the country and younger youth, leaders are disarming their leadership in resolving the issues and allowing the youth to embrace the rule of law as the hallmark of the country. Once you are destined for duty, you are also destined for leadership, role, and responsibility. Since the death of George Floyd, the January six insurrection, withdrawal from Afghanistan, the US southern border immigration crisis, and current legislative restructuring and government shutdown behavior, everybody disarmed their leadership role and responsibility to politics.

Due to this, leadership issues are compounding across the country. Social challenges over the past decade multiplied. Leadership issues and social challenges since the death of George Floyd, the January six insurrection, withdrawal from Afghanistan, the US southern border immigration crisis, and current restructuring and government shutdown issues are multiplying. Leaderships are passing on issues that come to the desk instead of resolving them. How do you define leadership, role, and responsibility? What kind of legacy are you leaving behind to the youth? How can you educate the youth about leadership, role, and responsibility by suggesting that leadership has no accountability? How can you tell your child that politicians have no accountability? If so, do they have a duty? If you have duty, you have accountability. Leadership descends and whatever leadership you show to the youth today descends on them.

Actions that affect the youth and public.

Over the last decade, I have experienced leadership actions negatively affecting the youth and the US public. I experienced George Floyd's death, the January 6 insurrection, the US quick withdrawal from Afghanistan, immigration issues at the US southern borders, and divisiveness in Congress. I also experienced police officer killings continuing across other states, people kneeling while the national anthem is sung, January 6 insurrectionists unfairly put in jail, disputes about election results, divisiveness within a political party, and divisiveness in Congress.

Besides this, I experienced the government ignoring mental health as the source of gun violence, Confederate monuments removed from public places, Congress shutting down the government at the time of enhancing and bridging foreign policy gaps, and a change of democratic culture across the country. If everybody across the nation will continue to follow democracy this way, how do you define leadership, role, and responsibility in the United States?

George Floyd and Police interventions

Since the death of George Floyd, officer killings increased. This time, it is not in Minneapolis but across the country. I would think that the protests that went on across the country and over the world about George Floyd's death were enough not to see any unlawful killings by officers in the country. But it was the beginning of officers wrongfully killing innocent people in the country. Officers have carried out killings upon killings and have put not only their bosses in the bad spot of law and policies, but also their families and the entire officers of the law enforcement professions.

This shows that the officers who killed George Floyd and the other officers who committed killings across the country are not connected. For separate scenarios but the same killings. They took someone's life. I would bet that all these officers who made bad decisions in killing innocent citizens were law enforcement officers who love the job and are willing to work and protect the community. They went through the same academy training as other officers did and got the same training skills, but they wrongfully ended someone's life while on duty. This was not a lack of training, but it was a lack of understanding of their leadership role and responsibility.

Understanding leadership role and responsibility.

Regardless of your knowledge and experiences, if you do not understand your leadership role and responsibility, you are most likely to drop a bowl. This is what happened to the Minneapolis police officers. The officers have training skills and experience, and are committed to the job, but they did not understand that their leadership role and responsibility were to protect George Floyd. Even as they pursued their duty to apprehend George Floyd, they did not understand their leadership role and responsibility after apprehending George Floyd. They unlawfully ended George Floyd's life. I will bet that these officers were knowledgeable and had enough experience to intervene and apprehend George Floyd, but they lacked leadership role and responsibility to save Floyd's life. This same behavior of Minneapolis police officers overshadowed many police officers across the nation to commit innocent killings. One thing about those police officers who committed innocent killings is that they love the job. They care about people. They also care about the community, but they lack understanding of leadership roles and responsibility to better carry their duty to the highest level of professionalism. Due to this, the public often jumps to the conclusion that all police officers are quick to kill. I strongly disagree with this conclusion. I will bet that when police officers understand their leadership role and responsibility, they will be safer than kill.

Police are passionate about duty.

Due to many police accidental killings across the country, the public does not see the sacrificial job of all police officers in the community. Police officers are committed to the people in the community. They will ensure that your calls are answered and officers are dispatched to save you. They will respond to any 911 calls at any time and anywhere, whether day or night. They work around the clock to prevent any worse thing happening to you. This is a passion that you can count on every police officer. A passion that police officers embraced as a hallmark of their job.

Police officers enforce the law regardless of the environment.

Therefore, law enforcement officers are dedicated to their work and certain about their duty to enforce the law safely and securely. While law enforcement officers are dedicated to the job, not every officer understands the leadership role and responsibility of the business. Due to this, some officers commit unlawful killings. The public calls them bad apple officers, but they are not because no officer does not wants a paycheck. What is true is that those officers lack understanding of not only the business leadership, role, and responsibility but also their own leadership, role, and responsibility of the business. These are the skills and resources that every officer needs at the time of any eventuality/confrontation during operations, rounds, or work time. Due to this lack of understanding, some officers do not know that their leadership role and responsibility is critical not only to promote professionalism in the law enforcement environment but also to promote trust in the public. The public expects accountability from law enforcement officers. Due to this, when one officer accidentally/unlawfully kills a citizen, the public rashes with protests against all officers. This is what happened in George Floyd's killing and all other unlawful killings across the country. It is critical to help officers set goals not only to enhance their knowledge in the business but also when on duty.

Setting goals on duty

Officers' relationships with the communities are infinite. The Officers are not limited to any community in any way. Therefore, officers' interactions in town must have a professional pattern of behavior in the town. This will show officers' long-term goals not only in the job but also in the area. Apart from 911 emergencies, every city is known for something that every officer can incorporate into the agenda. It could be a drug or crime. The officer can incorporate that as a goal and pursue it until it is achieved. In this way, the officer will have a perspective of what his/her daily routine will look like in a week, month, or year. This goal will help the officer to develop a positive bond with the community and the area targeting the population that is involved with crime and violence. In the absence of officers, setting a goal can result in an officer flattering around in the community with personal motives, instead. When I set up a goal to target violent population groups or groups that are causing trouble in the community, my leadership role and responsibility to achieve the goal kicks up. Whenever I engage with this population, I know what I need to do to keep myself and the environment safe using the skills, experience, leadership role, and responsibility. Knowing this will help me ensure that my leadership role and responsibility reflect my job and relationship in the community. These are some of the things that many officers often ignore in their daily operations. Your relationship with the community that you work for and the community that you live in is the same. Therefore, when you take your leadership role and responsibility for your duty, you will promote a safe and secure community without unlawful killings.

Ignoring victims' part of responsibility.

While the public often takes protests to the street for any police shooting and killing incidents, they often ignore the leadership role and responsibility of the victim. The victim's leadership, role, and responsibility leading to the action of the officer is the key element of the knot. When you assess the victim's leadership, role, and responsibility it helps not only understand the spectrum of the situation but also learn and analyze the sense of the interaction. It does not make the victim right or wrong, but it helps balance the question of the leadership roles and responsibilities of the subjects in question. There is no single person who is exempted from leadership roles and responsibilities of herself/himself or others. Leadership is not about being a manager in a grocery store, a governor, or the President of the United States, but you. You have a leadership role and responsibility to ensure that you take leadership roles and responsibility of yourself and others to the highest level of lives. There is always something that leads to officers' response. You have a leadership role and responsibility to avoid doing that thing, prompting officer intervention. This is the blank side of the public. While protests are critical to calling for justice in any policeinvolved killings, they also cover the sight of the public from reviewing victims' credentials and side of the story. Due to this, there is no public awareness about people taking their own leadership roles and responsibility to avoid any actions that prompt police intervention in the community.

Educate communities that misunderstand police officer's role.

It is critical to launch a law enforcement awareness campaign in the community that does not understand the police officer's role and enhance individual leadership roles and responsibilities. If the public understands the police officer's role in the community, they will not argue with the officer regardless of the situation. It will help balance misconceptions between police officers and public interactions to avoid accidental deaths. If officers and the public together show leadership roles and responsibility in their actions, there will be fewer accidental deaths or police killings in the community. Without the police and public understanding of individual or collective leadership roles and responsibilities, they will not have a break in how they communicate and act in the community. This is where society is misled. Society can jump into believing that communication is the key to balancing police and public altercations, but it is not the key. Because police and citizens can communicate at any time and exchange arguments on the street, but if they do not strike each other, nothing happens. But if they strike each other, regardless of the communication, something has happened. This is why leadership, role, and responsibility are critical in dialogue. It helps people to understand their leadership role and responsibility of the matter and assess their thoughts before action. Most of the police-citizen altercations that resulted in death happened because none of them showed leadership roles and responsibilities. They had communicated either directly or indirectly, but none of them showed to understand the other. This is where trust has become a problem when an officer dealing with a citizen or a citizen dealing with an officer,

Shine in your actions.

Allow your leadership to shine in your actions. Investing your time in understanding your leadership role and responsibility is critical to supplying or receiving good services in the community. Because it helps you act with clarity. When you show leadership role and responsibility in any altercation issue, it helps build trust with the opponent, understand the situation, and reduce the risk of pulling the trigger. Since the death of George Floyd, officers' relationship with the public has become worse due to trust and fear of losing life. Due to this, many killings continued. Trust and fear issues overshadowed citizens and officers to assess their encounter with each other in any risk situation. The officers fear that citizens might pull the trigger on them, while the citizens also feel that once officers kill George Floyd, they will also kill them. These are misconceptions that require the leadership role and responsibility of both officers and citizens to resolve. Trust and fear cannot be wiped off in the community between officers and citizens without them looking for a common ground to address it. One must take a stand, show leadership, and begin to rebuild trust with the other and wipe fear from the mind. It will help speed up the officer-citizen reunification initiative process.

Until officers and citizens understand the need to take leadership, role, and responsibility to the highest level of every altercation, fear and trust will cause them to engage in triggers and killings in the community.

The glance of President Trump's first government and the January 6 insurrection.

What did you know about President Trump's government? President Trump's government was one of the kinds in the country. The government gained more attention and favor across the country than any other government in my history. While the President is empowered by this enormous support of the country, he has overlooked on January 6 insurrection to shape his campaign. January 6 insurrection is a hiding threat, but the President does not want to admit that his government was involved in a political accident and encourage voters for a better leadership tomorrow. Without any question, the President was the Driver of the entire nation and addressed the protesters before they invaded the Capitol Hill. While this invasion escalated, the President and his government did nothing to stop it. As a result, people were killed, property was damaged, and insurrectionists now confined. While the President is gaining in every poll for the 2024 presidential elections, nobody knows the kind of government to expert if he will not denounce the January 6 insurrection and assure the public of better leadership tomorrow. Until the President tells the public that he will not pursue another January 6 insurrection, he owes a concern to the voters that the January 6 insurrection agenda is still active. In other words, how would you tell me that breaking into someone's home, damaging property, and killing people was nothing to worry about? If I do not understand what I did wrong, how would I positively change myself forward? What I want to say here is that if the President does not know that his government did not do enough to prevent the January 6 insurrection, how prepared is the President to lead another government and sustain democracy in the United States? As a citizen, how prepared are you to support the government and help sustain democracy in the country?

The glance of President Trump's first government and democracy.

Regardless of how President Trump gained support and favor across the country, he was not recruited to govern the country during the second term. Most of the people decided not to recruit the President for a second term. What went wrong in this picture? What was the problem then, and what is the problem now? Regardless of what happened then or now, the President did not concede losing the election and had never officially handed over power as usual. Whether this was coincidence, accident, deliberate, or anger, the President refused to concede. What kind of democracy is the President pursuing? To me, the pursuit of democracy is a sacrifice. A sacrifice that every citizen shared. Whether you are a Democrat, Republican, or Independent, your sacrifice is added up to yield the democracy that everybody enjoys every day across the country. While democracy is the hallmark of freedom, I believe there is no democracy without the people. People have the power to decide democracy. People also have the power to determine the government. If the President refused to concede the election to allow the democratic process to take root, what kind of leadership does the President expect to deliver to the American people this time? Will this be democratic leadership or another leadership? Due to the democratic process and the oath and constitutionality of the state, I live to believe that regardless of election results in the United States, the results often reflect the winner. Nobody questioned the results. However, the results were questioned. Because the President did not concede the results. If a democratic president in the United States refused to concede the election and had never officially handed over the power, how does the government sustain democracy? How do citizens keep democracy? While refusing to concede the election is politically fair, it is ethically concerned. In other words, how do you ease the January 6 insurrection's tension from the citizens even as it is considered a political accident?

January 6 insurrection

Over the next century, the memories of the January 6 insurrection will remain fresh in the minds of all Americans, not because of the lasting nightmare to citizens but because of the government's involvement in the act. Why? Because no government comes against itself. The biggest vision of every government is to protect the country and its citizens against internal and external threats. Every government's leadership has a role and responsibility to protect the nation. The leadership takes its leadership role and responsibility to the highest level of the government. They uphold democracy as the hallmark of the government. Regardless of adversities, the leadership of any government is not directly or indirectly involved in riots against the country. It is the heart of leadership roles and responsibility. However, when the leadership of the government directly or indirectly influences innocent citizens to commit insurrection, they lose the biggest vision of the government: leadership, role, and responsibility to protect the country. This is what I experienced on the January 6 insurrection. On the January 6 insurrection, I shared that the government, as the driver of the country, lost control of the government. It means that the leadership of the government slept behind the wheel. In other words, the government slept at the country's security gate, leaving the security doors open or unattended. To me, it was the darkest day in the United States. It will remain fresh in the minds of all citizens because the actions did not reflect the traditional culture of the United States' government. This does not mean the President was wrong in addressing the protesters, but it means the President did not do enough to prevent the riot at Capitol Hill.

January 6 insurrection is not a new culture.

While the January 6 insurrection nightmares are still fresh in the minds of all people across the country, politicians have embraced it as a new culture of leadership role and responsibility. Due to this, there is a hidden leadership and political tension not only in Congress but also across the nation. This political and leadership tension sends a wrong message to the youth that there is no accountability for leadership roles and responsibilities. It confuses the youth. How can leadership have no accountability? It is fair to say to the youth that the January 6 insurrection was an accident. It is not a new culture. If you consider the January 6 insurrection as a new culture of leadership role and responsibility, you are increasing the risk of another January 6 insurrection. You will not only miss the opportunity to assess it as an accident, but you will also miss the opportunity to assess the impact on the youth. The youth are learning from every behavior that the leadership of the country shows today, and they will act on it tomorrow. It means that when you consider the January 6 insurrection as an accident today, the youth will repair the damages tomorrow. However, if you consider the January 6 insurrection as a new culture today, the youth will consider a seizure of power tomorrow. Therefore, it is critical to let the youth know and understand that the January 6 insurrection was not only an accident but also a failure of leadership, role, and responsibility to prevent it. In this way, the youth will understand and take the leadership, role, and responsibility of the country to the highest level of government. Overall, it will help the youth to remain vigilant against political drummers that do not reflect the country's values and interests at home and abroad.

Consider the January 6 insurrection as a car accident.

Consider the January 6 insurrection as a real car accident and blame the President, not the insurrectionists. It will help the youth to understand the principles of leadership, role, and responsibility in an accident. In an accident, the driver takes responsibility. There is no driver causing an accident without taking a leadership role and responsibility for the accident. When you access and analyze a car accident, the driver must take accountability for the accident because the driver engaged in an accident. While this principle does not matter in politics, it does matter in leadership, role, and responsibility. This principle applies to every accident in every leadership role and responsibility in organizations, whether big or small, public or private. Based on this, when the leadership of the government is involved In any accident, such as the January 6 insurrection, you must assess and analyze the accident using the principles of resolving car accidents. These principles are critical in every leadership. In government, it forms the base upon which the leadership of the government works. It does help explain how critical leadership can transform government using these principles of accident. It means that the leadership of every government must work according to their leadership role and responsibility to avoid accidents. Regardless, when leadership takes part in an accident, it must not be politized as a new culture of leadership, role, and responsibility. It must be politicized as an accident. It is critically imperative not to use politics to cover political accidents caused by the political leadership of the government.

In other words, it is a political flood. The youth know the values of leadership, role, and responsibility, but they need to understand in practical terms to always allow leadership to balance with politics or overshadow it.

Politics overshadowed leadership.

While politics and leadership are intertwined, politics must not overshadow leadership in government, or else it will cause a political accident, as in the January 6 insurrection. To maintain a disciplined government, your leadership must overshadow politics or balance it to keep a productive leadership of the government. Politics is a misleading element. Once in power, politics can cause you to think wildly, undermine every authority, the integrity of your people, country, and the justice system of the nation, and grow hate and divisiveness among politicians and citizens in the country. Politics can influence you to lose sight of your leadership, role, and responsibility. Politics can tell you to deny your leadership role and responsibility, reject democracy, and keep power forever. Regardless, political influence can empower you to feel like the power of your leadership is personal, tear everybody down, or undermine the laws of the land and subject the youth to failure. But leadership will tell you to be mindful, pursue democracy, enhance leadership, and balance power. Leadership will tell you to uphold the nation, protect the integrity of your people and the nation, and work to inspire people to uphold democracy and the rule of law. To me, it is the dual role of leadership of government. But leadership, regardless of politics, would tell you to lead by example, have the youth in mind of your leadership, and take leadership as the hallmark of the country.

The greatness of a nation rests on leadership.

The country's greatness rests on its principles of leadership, role, and responsibility. It does not rest on a political party. Regardless of which political party is in power, the government's leadership must uphold leadership, role, and responsibility as the hallmark of the government to affect change. This is where many government leaders lose sight of the government. Often, when the leadership of a political party forms the government, they narrow down the vision to focus on what they can do to magnify the party, not the country. They will spend the entire four to eight years in the office magnifying the party by sticking to the party's principles while ignoring the country's leadership principles. To differentiate a party principle from the country's principles, you must understand the concepts of your family practices at home versus a community. In a home setting, certain behavior is considered normal practices, but in a community, you need to enhance such behavior to fit the normalcy of the community. This is why many government leaderships go off course and eventually end up with only one term in office, instead. Once your party forms the government, you must start doing things that matter to the country. Things that reflect the values of the country. Those things are beyond personal matters discussed at home. Even though personal matters appear normal in your home setting, they are not applicable in the community setting. When you incorporate personal matters from home with matters in the community, it misleads people. These are some of the reasons why the January 6 insurrection is still fresh in the minds of all Americas because the leadership did not differentiate matters between home and community.

Understand the difference between a political party and a country.

While a political party often forms the government, there is a vast difference between a political party and your country. Your home is your political party, and your community is the country. What matters for the United States today is not about the political party but the leadership of the country. Since the January 6 insurrection, divisiveness in the country's leadership, other leaders across political parties, and citizens are not balancing politics with leadership roles and responsibilities. Why? Because everybody is confused about a home and community or a party and country. Due to this confusion, nobody worries about which leadership fits which. Everybody is looking for the person they like, but not the person that qualifies for the job. Can a parent parenting at home be able to lead a community? Yes! A parent must enhance the parental leadership role and responsibility at home to fit the community's leadership role and responsibility. Because the leadership, role, and responsibility of a parent is different from that of the community. This principle applies to leadership in a political party and country. It means that when you move from your leadership role and responsibility in your political party to govern the nation, you must enhance your leadership skills to fit the governing leadership of the country. In other words, a political party is a home, and the country is a community. When you lose your home, you can always live in the community. But when you lose your community, you have no home. This is why it is critical for all citizens to be careful who they vote for in the leadership of the community. It is critical to also understand the levels of leadership role and responsibility when entering leadership. It will help you to enhance your skills each time you move from one leadership to the other. However, when you do not enhance your leadership skills while leading the community, you have an 80% possibility of collapse in your leadership. I believe this was one of many reasons why President Trump's government got frustrated and took it up to the January 6 insurrection. Therefore, enhance your leadership skills and ensure that your leadership reflects the values of the country such that the youth can learn from your legacy.

Passengers trust drivers, and citizens trust the government.

Passengers on the bus have no worries about how to get to their destination. Because they trust the driver behind the wheel, once they are on the bus, they know that the driver has a duty. They understand that the driver has leadership, role, and responsibility to drive them to their next destination. They have no worries about the driver's knowledge and skills to drive because they know every driver is certified to drive, or else the DMV will not give them a driver's license. Although this principle is true about drivers in the United States, it is critical to understand that it applies to every citizen trusting the leadership of the government. Citizens trust the leadership of the government because they know leadership has a duty. Like the passengers on the bus, the January 6 protestors/insurrectionists believed in President Trump's leadership. They trusted the leadership of his government and were sure that the President would drive them to the right destination.

However, the President drove the peaceful protestors into Capitol Hill, causing an accident. If this is the case, why are the passengers, the peaceful protesters, incarcerated? While you cannot avoid or deny the individual or collective leadership role and responsibility of the peaceful protesters or people involved in the January 6 insurrection, you can understand that they were passengers in the accident. Often, in accidents, small or big, authorities do not hold the passengers accountable but the driver. Because the driver drives the bus. In every car accident, if the driver is not at fault, there is no case against the driver and passengers. Regardless of this truth, politicians are motivated to have the insurrectionists incarcerated while the politicians involved in the accident are allowed to run for office. Regardless of how you viewed this, the insurrectionists were passengers. They never reached their destination.

Leaders are the drivers of the bus.

As a driver, I know how it is to be a driver in the United States. It all starts at the DMV. Learning a permit is the first step to start learning how to drive. Due to the enormous amount of drivers' roles and responsibilities on the road, you must invest your time and undergo driving practices with the driving school right after you receive the learning permit. They will invest their time and help you with the driving practice you need to get your license and be safe on the road.

They will train you how to control the steering wheel, understand how to use the signals or traffic lights, and professionally communicate with other drivers about your movements on the road. Overall, you will learn, understand, and pay attention to the road signs to be empowered behind the wheel. It is fascinating to understand that when you are certified and receive your driver's license, you are not guaranteed to be involved in an accident. Why? Because car accidents can happen to everyone in many ways. It could happen through the weather conditions, mechanical failure of the car, or through your fellow drivers. It could happen through the car beside you, behind you, or in front of you. However, when a car accident occurs, the driver takes responsibility. This principle applies to leadership roles and responsibility. It happened to President Trump and his government on the January 6 insurrection. The January 6 insurrection happened the same way as a car accident. However, in a car accident, the driver takes responsibility, but in that of the January 6 insurrection, only the passengers and the insurrectionists were held accountable. Regardless of how it happened, leaders must take leadership roles and responsibility to resolve issues rather than pass them on without resolution.

Do not stack in the January 6 insurrection holdback.

Regardless of how you feel about the January 6 accident, do not stack in the ambient feelings of the sentiment. It's true, in my view, that the divisiveness and hate that is engulfed in Congress derived from the holdbacks of the January 6 insurrection. Regardless of how you viewed it, many politicians are still in the mood to fight another January 6 insurrection. If you don't see this happening today or tomorrow, it will be too late to figure it out. My Dad often says that there is no smoke without fire. It means that the Congress cannot misbehave without the support of the community.

Due to this community support, many politicians and/or Congressmen and women are motivated to fabricate stories to redefine accidents in politics as a new way of leadership role and responsibility. It poses a concern to the youth. In other words, how are the youth educated in politics? As an educator, would you suggest to the youth that causing political accidents has no consequences in society? Take the burden off the youth. Painting the walls to cover the truth does not show leadership roles and responsibility. Regardless of your political accident, take your leadership, role, and responsibility to the highest level of your duty. It helps promote positive change not only in your profession and the government service but also in the community that you live in. It helps the youth to cheer up the joy of assuming leadership roles and responsibility in the personal self.

Shine in your leadership.

Until your leadership positively affects the people, your legacy will not be replicated in the community. Therefore, talk about the weaknesses of your leadership daily, or else you will not strengthen or balance them. I do not hear politicians discussing their leadership, role, and responsibility weaknesses. They talk about politics and how they can paint the walls of leadership roles and responsibilities to suit the political goals without thinking about the kind of legacy they are leaving behind.

The youth or future leaders are not looking for how much you play politics. They are looking at how you achieved in your leadership roles and responsibility. Regardless of party affiliation, your leadership must bring a positive impact to replicate. Your leadership does not only focus on people in your party but everybody in the aisle. Leadership must be influenced by these principles to take their leadership role and responsibility to the highest level of governance. Therefore, leadership runs on principles of leadership, role, and responsibility. When leaders allow politics to overshadow their leadership, they narrow their vision from helping the entire community to a home.

It is critical to know that politics must not overshadow your leadership, role, and responsibility. It must balance it. What matters for people today is their affiliation to the political party and the leadership. When you lead people to bring change, your leadership is remembered by the party and the entire nation. So, leadership is like a bus driver. A bus driver is well-trained to carry passengers from one destination to the other.

Leadership as bus drivers.

You are the driver of your leadership!

Leadership drives business the same way a bus driver drives people. While bus drivers drive people to their various destinations, leadership drives the people's aspirations to move business forward. For instance, when you become a law enforcement officer, you have become the driver of the community. Just as the bus driver transports people to their destinations, the law enforcement officer helps enhance the safety and security of the community. This principle applies to every leader, including individual citizens, a parent, teacher, lawyer, a Judge, the governor of the state or the President of the United States. It means that everybody has leadership roles and responsibilities.

You must show leadership where you are: leadership that brings positive change, whether socialist, consecutive, or independent. When you assume your leadership role and responsibility to lead people, you have become the driver of those people, whether you are an ordinary citizen or the President of the United States. You have a leadership role and responsibility to show those people that you love your job, are dedicated, and are committed to driving their aspirations in the right direction.

If you cannot assure them of anything, prove that you care about your leadership and are on the same bus as them. Prove to your passengers that you are heading in the right direction with your leadership, and ensure you arrive at the destination safely and securely. When you do, you will win their approval. When you become the President of the country, you have become the driver of the entire nation. The people of every state become your passengers, whether they are Democrats, Republicans, or Independents. No state has no Democrat, Republican, or independent. They are all your passengers. They are on your bus with you. You have the leadership, role, and responsibility to drive the aspirations of all these people across the country to the right destination, safe and secure. It shows leadership, role, and responsibility of your leadership.

Leadership and politics are intertwined.

Even though politics has become a fragmented art of leadership across the nation, politics is inevitable in leadership. Politics and leadership are intertwined. They must balance to meet the professionalism of leadership. Politics is used to shape leadership, while leadership is used to enhance politics. You need both leadership and political skills to dynamite your self. But leadership is the key. Without leadership, you cannot play professional politics. It means that you cannot pursue politics without showing leadership.

For the best, you can mechanize politics with your leadership role and responsibility to bring the positive change you need for your people. It's like the combination of coffee, sugar, and cream. It tests well. When you add sugar and cream to the coffee, you will experience the flavors of the drink. While the mixture suppresses the bitterness of the drink, you experience the best test of the drink. Leadership is like sugar and cream in coffee. It helps flavorists politics. While leadership and politics are intertwined, they can become inversely proportional when unbalanced. When you dominate politics in your self without leadership, you will miss the target or opportunity to serve your people well. This is what I experienced In the January 6 insurrection. Because the politics and leadership of the government did not balance, the government's actions went viral among the protesters. However, everybody blames the protesters because they don't see anything wrong with the government's leadership. It means that the protesters are citizens and have no representation in politics. However, politicians are using politics to shield their fellow politicians.

Politics and January 6 insurrection

If you doubt whether politics played a role in the January 6 insurrection, you are still in the hula hoop of politics. Politics played a role. Due to this, the Democrat and Republican leaders are suspending judgment on all politicians who were involved in the January 6 insurrection. None of them is talking about the behavior of the government's leadership, role, and responsibility in the act. Still, they are talking about the behavior of the protestors on Capitol Hill.

Due to this, politics has become the focal point of the pursuit of the January 6 insurrection. They have ruled out the behavior of the government's leadership, role, and responsibility in the action. It means that politicians are politically pursuing the January 6 insurrection accident. Due to this, they have reached the limit of proportionality in the pursuit. They cannot go any further. It means they cannot go forward or backward because President Trump is already in the air campaigning for the 2024 presidential elections.

Politically, nothing holds the President from moving forward with the campaign, regardless of the involvement in the January 6 insurrection. The President is not politically bound to reign for any office. Why? Because politics is a fragmented framework.

Due to this fragmentation of politics, political leaders are not held accountable but citizens. The protestors or insurrectionists are imprisoned while politicians and leaders who influenced the insurrection are enjoying themselves with their families. This is why politics played a role in the January 6 insurrection's accident. Whenever politics overshadow leadership roles and responsibilities, an accident occurs. This is why the January 6 insurrection is an accident. You cannot understand this until you view the January 6 insurrection as a car accident on the road.

Insurrection as an accident

While people think the January 6 insurrection was a plot to take over the government, I believe it was an accident. The leadership of President Trump's government was involved in a political accident. President Trump was the driver, and everybody involved was a passenger. I see this as a full charter bus driving towards Washington, DC on the interstate highway. Due to political cloudiness at that time, President Trump was overwhelmed in leadership, role, and responsibility and turned a head-on to Capitol Hill, causing the accident and fatalities.

Whether the nation recognizes this as an accident or not, politicians have already worked it out wrong. They have set free all their fellow politicians involved in the January 6 insurrection accident. However, they incarcerated the passengers, in this case, the insurrectionists. Currently, all the politicians who were involved in the January 6 insurrection, either directly or indirectly, are holding their jobs while President Trump is pulling ahead in polls for the 2024 presidential elections, but the insurrectionists are sitting in jail. It means that the nation fully supports President Trump and all politicians involved in the political accident.

However, not everyone went on the street supporting the protestors/ insurrectionists. Suppose you can understand that the January 6 insurrection accident is the same as a car accident on the road. In that case, you can agree that all the insurrectionists or protesters were passengers and must not take responsibility for the accident. How would you feel if the driver in the accident was set free and the passengers of the accident were incarcerated? In an accident, if you cannot find anything wrong ethically, Biblically, legally, socially, and/or politically to hold the driver accountable, you do not have any reason to hold the passengers accountable. Why? Because passengers cannot drive themselves.

Passengers trust drivers as well as citizens trust the government.

Passengers on the bus have no worries about how to get to their destination. Because they trust the driver behind the wheel, they know that the driver has a duty once they are on the bus. They understand that the driver has leadership, role, and responsibility to drive them to their next destination. They have no worries about the driver's knowledge and skills to drive because they know every driver is certified to drive, or the DMV will not give them a driver's license. In comparison, this principle is true about drivers in the United States; it is critical to understand that it applies to every citizen trusting the government's leadership.

Citizens trust the government's leadership because they know leadership has a duty. Like the passengers on the bus, the January 6 protestors/insurrectionists believed in President Trump's leadership. They trusted his government's leadership and were sure that the President would drive them to the right destination. However, the President drove the peaceful protestors into Capitol Hill and caused an accident. If this is the case, why are the passengers, the peaceful protesters, incarcerated? While you cannot avoid or deny the individual or collective leadership role and responsibility of the peaceful protesters or people involved in the January 6 insurrection, you can understand that they were passengers in the accident. Often, in accidents, small or big, authorities do not hold the passengers accountable but the driver because the driver drives the bus.

In every car accident, if the driver is not at fault, there is no case against the driver and passengers. Regardless of this truth, politicians are motivated to have the insurrectionists incarcerated while the politicians involved in the accident are allowed to run for office. Regardless of how you viewed this, the insurrectionists were passengers. They never reached their destination.

No political accident is guaranteed.

A political accident is like a car accident, and it's not guaranteed even if you have many years of experience. In a car accident, police officers respond to the scene to assess and clear the site for traffic. They come simultaneously with the fire service personnel and ambulances to ensure that any life-threatening issues or injuries are attended to immediately. As soon as the site is cleared, all matters are over. Drivers who caused the accident are given a citation to appear in court. This same principle applies to the political accident I experienced on the January 6 insurrection. Once the legislators decided on the January

6 insurrection issues, there should be no anger, divisiveness, personal or political drumming still exist in Congress. All matters about self-interest should be over in Congress, allowing Congressmen and women to work together for the nation's interest. It shows the leadership, role, and responsibility of the Congress. It also shows leadership at home and abroad. It is the heart of leadership. However, the Congress is yet to stay divided even within each political party.

Do not tear the country down.

The divided Congress has taken heads in politics about party differences and the holdbacks of the January 6 insurrection. Whatever you see happening in Congress today is also happening in the community. The behavior of Congress is clouding the entire country. I used to hear my Dad tell me that "when two horses are fighting, grass suffers." I did not understand what my Dad meant when he told me this, but today, I understand him. I understand that what is going on in Congress reflects what is happening in the community.

The Congress is doing what the community wants them to do. The Congress does not have power by itself. The community gives Congress power. If what is happening in Congress today is in the interest of the community, where is citizens' leadership role and responsibility to protect the nation? It takes only one person to tear the country down. The strength of the country does not rest on how tall and giant you are but the unity and morale of the citizens. You have the leadership role and responsibility to bring change in Congress to your community and help prepare the youth for a better future in leadership role and responsibility. It's the heart of leadership.

Use your leadership to influence change.

How do you use your leadership to influence positive change? Does positive change come from the sky, sea, or from the land? It comes from you. You are the leader of change. In the same way, you learn from others, so others learn from you. No person can influence positive change without taking leadership, role, and responsibility for their duty. I do not expect leaders to be 100% always correct to impact a change, but I expect leaders to apologize if they are wrong or apologize if they do not mean it. This is how leadership can connect with people and influence change.

The transparency of leadership draws people's attention to leadership roles and responsibilities. Because people can learn to connect with the leadership and team up with them, the knowledge learned is transferable. People can always reference what they learned and use it to model the youth and prepare them for the future. The youth often use experience learned from past leadership to enhance their leadership. The young always learn from the old. It has always been how leadership is structured. Your leadership role and responsibility set an example of the legacy you are leaving behind. Therefore, your leadership does not only influence the present, but it also influences the future. It is how leadership influences positive change.

Leadership can be seen as a common chain that influences a pull in a towing truck. Without a chain, towing vehicles cannot pull a car. The chain connects cars, influencing one car to pull the other. Be a chain in your leadership.

Leadership as a bridging element

Leadership is a bridging element that influences change in society just as the chain influences pull in a towing truck. For a towing truck to tow a car, a chain is always recommended. The leadership of the towing company ensures that they have chains in towing trucks to pull cars. The chain bridges the gap between the two vehicles and influences the pull. Without the chain, towing companies cannot do business. This same principle applies to leadership.

Leadership is a bridging element in our society. Without leadership, there would be no role and responsibility to influence positive change. Leadership bridges the gaps in society and influences positive change. Naturally, this implies that leadership has accountability for the duty. No single person can influence a positive change in society without being accountable for leadership and bearing responsibility. Accountability comes from your leadership role, and you bear responsibility as a result.

This is what I did not experience on the January 6 insurrection accident. I did not see the leadership of the government taking leadership, role, responsibility, or accountability for the accident.

The accident showed that the leadership of the government did not bridge the leadership role and responsibility gaps of the nation. It also means that the actions of the government's leadership did not influence positive change, as the chain in a towing truck influences positive change. Instead, the leadership of the government broke the chain that holds the country together.

Due to this, the country is divided and vulnerable. This divisiveness and vulnerability are clouding the country, yet the majority are embracing it as a new culture of leadership, role, and responsibility. If this is the case, how do you define leadership, role, and responsibility in the United States? Leadership is a bridging element that influences change in society just as the chain influences pull in a towing truck. If this evidence is inevitable, the question arises – what does leadership mean to you in the United States?

Help bridge the leadership gap.

Does leadership mean a manager in the grocery store, the governor of the state, or the President of the United States?

No.

Leadership is you.

You can help bridge the leadership gap! You are leading the country right from your home, car, work, or business, or where you find yourself. Your behavior affects the country. Your behavior decides your part of the country's leadership role and responsibility. Instead of judging the leadership of the country, judge your own behavior and critically evaluate whether you are pursuing the right leadership, role, and responsibility in supporting the nation.

While assessing your own leadership, role, and responsibility, remind yourself that America is the United States. America is not about Democrats or Republicans, Blacks or Whites, citizens and noncitizens, but the United States of America.

Unity is the backbone of the country's leadership, role, and responsibility.

Ask yourself the following questions: If leadership is you, what are you holding back in your leadership? Are you leading divided or united? Where do you stand with your leadership role and responsibility for the country? What does leadership and responsibility mean to you in America? How are you living the January 6 insurrection? How are you standing up for youth? How are you living the united values of the country?

Take your leadership, role, and responsibility judiciously and figure out the answers to these questions.

Blame the government, not insurrectionists.

The leadership of the nation is not only helping bridge the gaps of people or pulling them forward but also leaving them with a legacy that is transferable. Society lives on legacy. A positive legacy spikes people to pursue better opportunities and achieve better goals. So, the leadership of the nation does not have to engage in behavior that ordinary people do.

The leadership of the country is the light of the country. Everybody looks up to leadership as role models. Since leaders are to be held accountable, you must blame the government that influenced the January 6 insurrection but not the insurrectionists. The insurrectionists were peaceful protesters until they were influenced by the government to invade Capitol Hill.

However, Congress changed these narratives, giving 100% of the support to the government and putting vulnerable citizens in jail. As a result, many people were misled and began to think that the behavior of the government on insurrection was a new culture of leadership. The government influenced insurrection. This legacy is not replicable as it is not a legacy that the youth and future leaders can look up to.

It is not too late to repair the damages of the January 6 insurrection, but it is too late to drag it on. It undermines the values of leadership, role, and responsibility. In other words, it undermines the integrity of the country. Whichever way is credible, it is good to be aware that leadership descends, and the youth are susceptible to information.

Whatever you tell the youth today, they are going to act on it tomorrow. What is your pass-on story to the youth about the January 6 insurrection accident? What would you say to the youth about the reactions of the Democrats, Republicans, Independents, and the entire population of the country about the January 6 insurrection? The entire country was divided. Nobody was in accord with each other about how they could manage the accident in a way to educate the youth about the tradition of American leadership, politics, and the rule of law. This shows how vulnerable the country is in passing on the legacy of insurrection to the youth and future generations.

Fate is not leadership.

What many politicians are accustomed to in leadership today is fate, not leadership. Fate has become the focal point of leadership or politics across society. What people do not know is that fate and leadership are distinctly different. While fate helps you to stick around in politics and pursue your career, it is not dependable. When you believe in fate or yourself in managing the affairs of your authority without assuming your leadership role and responsibility, you are going to miss the opportunity to liberate your people in your authority because leadership is not about fate or personal self but about people.

While fate is the driving force that leads people to love themselves, their homes, community, and nation, having fate does not mean you can lead your people. Regardless of how fatefully you love your home, community, or country, if you do not balance it with leadership, role, and responsibility, you are going to mislead your people into the jungle.

I see this happening everywhere every day in society. I see leaderships, as well as individual persons, turn to relying on fate, instead of the leadership role and responsibility. As a result, divisiveness in Congress and within political parties still exists. Instead of working united, they are working divided. In the same way, many leaders across the nation are overshadowed by fate. They act racially, trying to deceive the public that racism exists in the United States. Those people are the reason why racial injustice is still mitted in society. It's fate, not leadership, even if you feel like it. What you need to know is that exercising fate means you are avoiding leadership roles and responsibility. You are living the values of the country even if you feel like it.

Balance your fate with leadership.

Balance your fate with leadership. If you do not understand leadership, regardless of your fate, you are going to mislead your people into a jungle. Many people are misled into a jungle by the leaderships that serve them. Many people today are depending on fate to govern rather than dual leadership, role, and responsibility. It is hard to imagine how people are accustomed to fate leadership, but it is not hard to figure it out. In business, you can see the struggle.

They have no patience for anything. They have no patience to model themselves and their staff. No strategy to develop training for staff to enhance their knowledge. They will fire people, including those in the team with them. You will see many people resign from their positions. Many staff members will be deceived to plot against other people. There will be a whole lot of political and leadership tension in the business.

However, when you assume your leadership role and responsibility, you have a good grip on the business. You will understand that your leadership role and responsibility have already been outlined. Your duty is not only to allow everybody to assume their role but also to encourage collaboration to ensure that all actions are communicated back to you in a professional and consistent manner. It helps you to create a healthy environment for everybody to function as a team, both individual and collective. This is how fate balances with leadership. It means that you are using evidence-based approaches in your practices because you are depending on outlined principles of leadership, role, and responsibility.

You are destined to lead, not to mislead.

While many leaders are accustomed to fate, they miss the opportunity to balance their fate with leadership, role, and responsibility. This is what everybody is destined to do. You are destined to balance your fate with leadership, role, and responsibility. You do not need to hold a job to assume leadership, role, and responsibility. Right from your bed, you have a duty to assume your leadership, role, and responsibility to balance your fate with your daily duties. It will lead to leadership roles and responsibility in a way that helps balance your family and community leadership. Based on this, you must pursue your daily routine with a theory that people can understand you better.

If people cannot understand your theory, you must explain it to them. It will help people make up their minds about whether they should work for the vision. It will help them decide to work for you. Because they know it and understand it. I did not see this with President Trump's government. While President Trump's government inspired many people to follow him, it also misled many people who did not understand his philosophy. President Trump's government centered on deciduous philosophy.

Deciduous philosophy.

Deciduous philosophy is a philosophy that is stigmatized by people aiming at short-term goals and encourages temporal relationships while maximizing profit when dealing with people. This philosophy has not been studied, but it was developed by my Dad when he observed and analyzed the behavior of farmers during harvesting season in a small community in the Upper East Region of Ghana.

During harvesting season, market men and women come to the area to buy fresh produce from farmers right from the farm. The market women and men created the impression that they were helping the farmers by coming to them to buy the produce instead. Due to this impression, many farmers would sell all their produce within four months of harvest and live with nothing to eat. However, the market women and men will preserve the produce they buy from the farmers the entire time. A few months down the road, the market women and men will bring back the produce, double the price, and sell them back to the farmers and make a profit. During this time, the farmers don't have cash. They would sell their life stock to buy back what was already theirs. Based on this, the farmers were always struggling to make ends meet.

My Dad described this behavior as deciduous because farmers were stigmatized by this theory aiming at short-term goals and encouraging temporal relationships, while the market men and women maximize profit dealing with them. In my opinion, this is the philosophy that President Trump is pursuing.

Many who did not understand the President's philosophy were not successful in his government. They were fired, resigned, deceived to invade Capitol Hill, kneeled while the national anthem was sung, labeled as hate groups, and put to jail while the President was amassed both popularity and wealth.

Labeled protesters

The individual groups who were stigmatized by President Trump's deciduous philosophy were deceived to take part in the riots at Capitol Hill. They were labeled as 'Hate groups' and put to jail while the President campaigns for the 2024 presidential elections. No matter how the protestors were labeled, I believe they were good people who were stigmatized by President Trump's deciduous philosophy. I have never heard about any of these groups attacking the United States government at that level.

Regardless of how these groups of people hate others in the community, they have never mobilized against the government at that level. I believe that these groups were out to protest the election results just as everybody else does in any protest. However, they were influenced by President Trump's government and did not fully understand the President's philosophy.

But how did this happen?

Or rather, more importantly, *why* did this occur?

The answer is pretty simple. What else would you do if the President of the United States cheered you up in the middle of a protest and said, "You are special?" Would you not be drenched in excitement and act out of mind in support of whatever the President asked you to do? Let nothing surprise you about how the President failed the protesters on the January 6 insurrection.

I see these people as good people indeed because they love the President and have the best interests of our country at heart. These people, who are now so crudely labeled as 'Hate groups,' have families, spouses, and children. They care for their homes, communities, jobs, and businesses. These are all features of good citizens. They have good motives to be proud of the President and protest on the street just as everybody else does.

The President missed the opportunity to model them into leadership, role, and responsibility of the country. Instead, he subjected them to insurrection, causing them to storm Capitol Hill, breaching the building, damaging properties, and fatalities. As a result, the President misled innocent citizens into jail.

Failed pathway

While President Trump's government misled the insurrectionists to attack Capitol Hill, he did not create a pathway for them. A way that people from the organization will be seen as a role model. In every organization or group of people, the leadership always stands out with leadership, role, and responsibility for the group. The members of the group often show their commitment by collaborating and giving support to the leadership, just as the insurrectionists did to President Trump. The group is known for what they believe and do. It is who they are in society. Regardless of their aspirations in the group, their expectation for new growth is always high. They are never limited to any positive vision and advancement.

They are only limited by their vision to try. They know that when you limit yourself to a small vision, you have little success. In my opinion, this is how President Trump's government viewed the insurrectionists. In my view, the President limited the vision of the insurrectionists by subjecting them to insurrection. It was not on purpose. But it was how fate played a role in leadership.

I believe that the President did not know that his leadership in the country was a success for people who love him. He did not know that if he leads the country responsively, taking leadership, role, and responsibility of the government diligently, he will create a positive image not only for his members, but also for the entire country. Due to this disconnect in vision, the President did not create a good image for the insurrectionists. He subjected them to jail, causing people to think that they were hate groups.

Destiny

The insurrectionists were labeled as hate groups not because of who they were but because of what they did on Capitol Hill. They invaded Capitol Hill, damaged the property, and breached the building. As a result, people were killed and injured. It was what they did, but that was not who they were as people. Individually or collectively, they are citizens of the United States. They understand that the country is the mother of democracy across the globe. They are also parents, community members, and leaders.

The insurrectionists are destined to lead the country in many ways. They are destined to be an entrepreneur, managers, governors, and/or the President of the United States. While all these opportunities lie before them, they look up to the President as a role model. But the President did not see these people as an asset or in the lens of leadership, role, and responsibility. However, he saw these groups of leaders as a tool to deploy for his own motives.

The President missed the exit to direct the insurrectionists to a peaceful protest and assure them of the potential to become future leaders. It was also where the President allowed his fate to overshadow his leadership, role, and responsibility. Due to this twit of leadership, the insurrectionists were subjected to and labeled as hate groups in the country. They were persecuted and then thrown into jail.

However, these so-called hate groups were not destined to hate anybody!

In other words, nobody is destined to hate people. You can decide to hate people, but it's your choice. It is not what you are destined to do in life. Therefore, it is critical to understand that when you positively assume your leadership, role, and responsibility, it gives you the perspective to see people under your leadership as assets, not tools. In this way, you will help them discover their potential and model them to pursue goals that matter not only for themselves but also for society.

Personality

While President Trump has the greatest leadership personality at the time, he is not humble about it. To be humble does not mean you should worship people, but to take your leadership, role, and responsibility to the highest level of your society. Develop a theory that resonates with the vision of the nation and Western World that balances with the vision of the non-Western world.

However, the President holds onto a deciduous philosophy that is stigmatized by people aiming at short-term goals and encourages temporal relationships while maximizing profit dealing with citizens. It means that the President does not encourage long term goals. While the President could use his personally to unite the Democrats, Republicans, and Independents, he chooses divisiveness over unity.

Due to this, divisiveness is born in Congress and gradually clouding the country. Following these matters, it is critical to understand that the President did not humble himself in leadership. However, when the President humbled himself, God would exalt him and lift him in honor (James 4:10) and equip him with knowledge, understanding, and wisdom to serve the nation. This is Biblical. It is not political. But when you ignore Biblical values in your leadership, you are going to lack the most precious resources you need to govern your people. Regardless of your leadership experience as President, be religious, assume your leadership role and responsibility, and embrace Biblical values in your leadership. With this, the President's personality will yield a positive outcome not only for the nation but also for the Western and non-Western worlds. It's the heart of leadership.

Business As The New Dialogical Means For the Western and Non-Western Worlds

What I thought was President Trump's dialogical means to bridge the Western and Non-Western with business turned out to be a hula hoop. It means that the President did not achieve the spread of business as a dialogical means of uniting the Western and nonWestern worlds. The President met with Russian and North Korean leaders, but there was no mutual relationship set up about business. To me, a mutual relationship about business with the non-westerners is when the leadership of the US and non-westerners agree to allow businessmen and women to engage in business across the countries without conflicts. For example, US and China trade relationships enable businessmen and women across both countries to trade without conflict. If the President had mutually engaged with these two leaders enough, the Russian President would not have engaged in a war.

Furthermore, US businessmen and women will be doing business in North Korea. I believe the ongoing nuclear testing in North Korea is not a sign of aggressiveness. But a sign of appeal. I think the North Koreans have lived in isolation for many years, not because they don't want to socialize with other countries, but because other countries are not open to them enough, partly because there are no ongoing diplomatic business talks with the North Koreans.

While it is too late to reverse Russians' mission from wars abroad, it is not too late to dialogue with the North Korean leader about business proposals. At this moment in time, the North Korean leader needs businesses to liberate the country. This pending relationship is an overdue job of the US leadership. US leadership has not yet finished their job with the North Korean leader. The two countries must engage in business, if nothing else. If President Trump was quick to start an indirect relationship with the North Korean leader, then the US leadership must be quick to start a direct relationship with North Korea. It is the pursuit of democracy, leadership, role, and responsibility.

Democracy, Western and Non-Western Worlds

While democracy is born in the Western World, it can grow in the non-Western world. Every one of the non-westerners that I spoke with said they are enjoying freedom here in the United States. However, they said they WORRY about their families back in their countries every day. They wish to remain anonymous not because they do not want to talk but because they do not know how the information will reflect on them in their countries. Based on this, I believe that citizens in non-Western worlds love democracy, but the leaders don't because they have the desire to hold on to power for as long as they can.

The Western world has a leadership role and responsibility to reach out to non-Western leaders with democratic dialogue. Engage them with the dialogical practices of democracy. It will help them make a better to pursue democracy. Democracy does not take power away from leadership, but it enhances power to decently government the people. Power comes from the people. When you give people the freedom to pursue life, they will provide you with the power to continue governing them. Therefore, democracy is not a one-way street. However, it is a circle of leadership roles and responsibility of the government and citizens. The non-western nations are welcome to this circle of leadership role and responsibility. It will help reduce power tension among citizens. It is the heart of leadership.

Divisiveness, Anger, And Hate Are Born in Congress

Nothing worries me about the leadership roles and responsibilities of the Congress than the divisiveness, anger, and hate that are born in the United States Congress. Once they are born, they will crawl and grow up into the next generation of leadership. Leadership descends, and I worry that some Americans might use this divisiveness, anger, and hate leadership of the Congress as a new culture of pursuing politics. It is Biblically proven that "When a kingdom is divided against itself, that kingdom cannot stand" (Mark 3:24-26).

Whatever is Biblically proven is real and cannot politically be corrected. Therefore, divisiveness, anger, and hate of any kind among the Congressmen and women in America is not political. It is personal. It affects not only the moral values of our men and women in uniform, but also it impacts all Americans.

I believe that divisiveness, anger, and hate destroy the political infrastructure of the country and put the nation at risk of vulnerability. The nation must support the founding principle of the country, the United States of America. The growing divisiveness, anger, and hate in Congress is an obvious reflection of how the communities are divided. If this is what is going on in the community, how is the country united? Without a question, it is time to mask the country. It is time for every citizen to take their leadership role and responsibility above divisiveness, anger, and hate. It is time to replace the Congress and to open our government.

End Government Shutdown Politics in Congress

While government shutdown politics has become a political tool for each political party to use against the other in the United States Congress, it lacks leadership roles and responsibility. A government shutdown, in my definition, is a failure of the legislative branch of government to pass the key government bills that keep the government open.

If the legislative branch of government refuses to pass the key bill of the government, they are suggesting a shutdown of the government. Regardless of politics, the Legislative branch should not subject the government to a shutdown. The government of the United States of America must not be subjected to shutdown.

Not only does this show weakness in leadership, role, and responsibility of the country, but it also has a negative impact on the young politicians in the country. It sends a dull signal to our enemies abroad. It does not reflect the leadership role and responsibility of the country abroad. The United States of America is United. It means that whatever you do in your person should reflect this unity. To me, it is the core principle of the country. It is no doubt that the founders of this country had this in mind. The country was formed not only to serve the world but also to lead and promote democratic leadership across the world.

The United States As the World's Democratic Leader

The United States of America is the world's democratic leader.

Without the US, democracy in many countries will fall out. Due to this, leadership across the country must develop this mindset as they serve as role models for the younger generation. It is critical to allow this awareness to bear fruit not only in all leaders of the country but also bear fruits in the youth today instead of tomorrow.

If you do not embrace the country as the world democratic leader today, tomorrow it will be too late. Considering the January 6 insurrection, the withdrawal from Afghanistan, the border immigration crisis, and the behavior of the legislative branch in subjecting the government to a shutdown during the critical moment of enhancing and bridging foreign policy gaps, I worry about the way leadership is recruited in government and the community. Nobody sees weaknesses of leadership in any way in anybody, even when weaknesses are experienced in leadership.

What has become common in the community today is political entitlement and stigma. Once you belong to the same political party as me, your weaknesses are covered. Whether in Congress or the community, you have my vote. Nobody cares about how these practices affect the youth.

What my Dad used to tell me was, "When you continue to cover your child's mistakes at home, you are going to collect the body on the street." My Dad would tell me this whenever he corrected any of my wrongdoings. What my Dad wants to put across here is that when you do not correct your child at home, you are not making your child a better person in the community. Based on this, the public must recruit leadership that understands the country's role in democracy and the rule of law and is able to promote such leadership across the nation. It will positively impact the youth and prepare them for a better America.

In God, we trust (The US)

While the US motto "In God we trust" is widely honored by drivers on license plates across the United States, it is barely honored in the US Congress. The Congress does not honor the motto, in God we trust. They honor politics.

What are you honoring in your person? Who are you trusting in your leadership? Are you trusting in people or God? It is hard to honor people. Because people are earthly, yet they do not understand earthly things (John 3: 12).

The earthly things that are practiced in Congress today are divisiveness, anger, and hate. These practices in Congress are clouding the communities causing people to think that divisiveness, anger, and hate are good cultural practices. They are not. While it is hard to honor people, it is not hard to trust in God. God is not a politician.

Regardless of your leadership, trusting in God reflects everything: Religion, politics, and government. The God we knew yesterday is the God we know today and will be the God we know tomorrow (Hebrews 13:8). God loves everybody.

God loves Blacks, Whites, Christians, Muslims, Jews, Arabs, and everybody you can mention. God also loves Democrats,

Republicans, and Independents. This description of God reflects the motto "In God we trust" and the vision of the United States of America to stay united.

Do not live here in the United States and still be an enemy to the country. Regardless of your holdback, the Congress has a holdback. Also, everybody in the country has a holdback. It is natural to have a holdback, but it is also natural to show leadership in your holdback and ensure that you do not allow that to overshadow your leadership. The motto says, "In God we trust." While divisiveness, anger, and hate are clouding the Congress and communities, you have a leadership role and responsibility to stop them by casting your vote to recruit people who are willing to promote unity.

Building a Strong America

To build a strong America is not only a huge privilege and opportunity but also a sacrifice. It is not just the duty of men and women in uniform but also you. It requires your leadership role and responsibility. You have a duty in your leadership to ensure that the truth is said and practiced.

If you don't do it, who is going to do it?

So, help build a strong America. Do not promote hate, anger, and divisiveness as a culture of leadership. Engage in dialogue and reflect on issues that matter for the country: Health, economy, education, and foreign policy. Maintain the values of the country: Leadership, role, and responsibility.

Look for common grounds where every American will love to collaborate with you in a unified way to make America great. Be sensitive to issues that genuinely affect the country. Develop trust and confidence in the system, but do not trust in yourself. Trusting in the self is fate.

I believe that not even a single person in America would act stupidly to destroy the nation, but I understand that fate is different from leadership. If you do not understand leadership, regardless of how fateful you want to lead your country, you will end up misleading the people. It is the kind of leadership I experienced during President Trump's government, where citizens were misled to kneel while the national anthem was singing, to attack Capitol Hill, or to kill George Floyd. To help build a strong America goes beyond fate. It requires you to assume duty from where you are and take your leadership role and responsibility to the highest level of your home and community.

The pandemic helped to rethink leadership as light.

The COVID-19 pandemic was not only considered the deadliest pandemics of the 21st century but it also enabled society to rethink leadership as the light of the society. The COVID-19 pandemic was a test for all leaders not only here in the United States but also across the world. Leadership that turns its light off on its people did not survive another election, but leaders that turn their lights on their people are still in power.

What I want to put across here is that when you are elected to an office of any level, you are entrusted with the control of the country's light switch. You are given the privilege to switch the light of the country off and on according to the ability of your leadership. Your leadership can decide to switch the light on to liberate people with resources and opportunities to succeed or switch the light off and put people in the dark, wiping them up with division, hate, and death.

The COVID-19 pandemic caught every leadership across the world in a surprise. Because there was no vaccine to fight the covid, due to this, many people died in hospitals, while others died at home because there were no hospital beds for admittance. The dead statistics rise every day. Covid patients in the hospital beds caught up in the hospital without their families.

It was total chaos. However, every country approached this COVID19 pandemic differently. Leadership that approached the COVID19 pandemic well left the leadership light on for their people. They did not undermine the pandemic. They were honest with the people about the COVID-19 threat and collaborated with the science communities until the vaccine was ready to liberate the people. Based on this, they are still in power. But leaders that switched off their leadership light on their people downplayed politics, undermined the pandemic, and passed on their leadership roles and responsibilities to others instead. These leaders did not pass the test, they did not survive the election, and they were not in power.

Sign of good leadership during COVID-19

First, the leadership of every government that switched on their leadership lights for their people during the COVID-19 pandemic was present with all their people even though the vaccine was not ready to liberate the people. They spoke faith to the people. Assured them of covid vaccine. They made their people understand that the pandemic was a challenge to everybody, but the scientists are working on developing a vaccine to control the spread of the covid. Leadership collaborated with the scientific and medical community experts from his/her cabinet and communicated the news to the public. Because of the consistent collaboration of the scientific and political teams, the news media fed genuine information. Based on this, the public receives the right information from the media all the time about the covid, the vaccine, and the government. The government presented the true picture of the pandemic to the people and assured the people that they were all together in the pandemic.

Leadership during crisis

The leadership of the government did not only switch their leadership lights to the people, but also, they also understood only one principle: people are happy when a child is born, but people mourn when a child is dead. When a child is dead, it is not an enjoyable time to be happy. During the pandemic, many families were mourning the loss of their loved ones. It was not time for politics. It was time for family. It was time for the leadership of every government to connect with the families that lost their loved ones. It was time for the government to encourage the entire community that the government is with them; the vaccine will be here to limit the spread of COVID-19 and tell the public to follow social distancing, wear masks, and wash their hands according to the CDC guidelines. When the leadership of the government is visible, connecting with the public, and telling them the truth about the COVID-19 vaccine, the public will not only build trust in the government but also they will develop a positive mindset about the vaccine.

Governments that left their people in the dark during COVID-19.

The governments who switched off their leadership lights off their people during the COVID pandemic were not present for their people. They were sleeping. They left their people in the dark, scared, confused, and desperate because there was no light. The leadership did not care or worry about the spread of the pandemic, how it kills people, and how families are mourning their loved ones. Even though the government knew people were in the dark, they were not worried about the safety or health of their people, whether people were sick or dead. The people had no plan or direction on where to go to be safe. People had no access to resources to help themselves. Because the governments will not change their stands, switch the lights on, or give people the support they deserve, many people perished their lives with COVID-19. It is odd when the government is not present with people during crises. The government said once leadership is healthy, safe, and free from COVID-19, everything is fine with the people.

Leadership promoting self-reliance during a pandemic.

The government did not only abandon its people but also understood only one principle: self-reliance or being on your own. The pandemic is not a personal or private issue. The pandemic is a public issue. The government must address the issue because the pandemic requires a higher level of collaboration due to the number of resources needed to engage experts to develop a vaccine. The philosophy of Self-reliance applies to personal or secluded settings only when the country is in normalcy, the economy is booming, jobs are created, and people are busy working and taking care of their families. In the pandemic, when the government campaigned on self-reliance, the leadership abandoned people. Because people will lack the resources they need to take care of themselves in their homes and communities, there will be complete chaos in the country. People will be divided into many class groups. The class group that is well-to-do may support self-reliance, but how many of these well-to-do class groups can form a majority to help the government win an election? When the government turns against its people, it has switched off its leadership light on them. It is what I learned about leadership.

COVID-19 pandemic in the US.

In the United States, the COVID pandemic did not only become a political battle, confusion, and nightmare, but it was also undermined. Leadership at that time did not understand that they have a role and responsibility to reason with the people in any situation, whether COVID-19 pandemic or war. Therefore, they did not embrace the options to be present with their people during the pandemic and seriously take their role and responsibility to the highest level during the pandemic. Due to this, they missed the opportunity to encourage people to be strong, provide them with the approaches to resolve daily issues while collaborating with the scientific/medical experts about vaccines. However, it was confusing here in the United States to hear crisscrossed information from leadership that COVID was not a threat while undermining the vaccine. Even though scientists developed covid vaccine for people to help limit hospitalization and deaths, people were scared to take it. Because they were frustrated and confused. These frustrations and confusion were also experienced in protesters who were protesting the systemic racism kneel while the national anthem was sung just to get the government's attention for intervention.

Kneeling on the national anthem as a means of protest.

As many people failed in many attempts to get President Trump's attention to COVID-19 and systemic racism issues across the country during his government, they kneel on the national anthem. While citizens kneeled during the national anthem to get the President's attention to intervene in the pandemic of systemic racism and COVID-19, they were hurting the country just as the President was hurting the nation. There was no leadership, role, and responsibility. What went wrong here is that the failure of the President to take leadership, role, and commitment of his government to protect the nation is not an excuse to kneel on the national anthem. Please, stop! Please, don't do it! Please, stand up for the national anthem. Stand up for your country. Take leadership, role, and responsibility of the country to the highest level of your leadership.

National anthem unites.

The national anthem unites the country. Wherever the national anthem is sung, everybody rises with leadership, role, and responsibility. The morale of people becomes high because they are ready to do what matters for themselves, their organization, or the country to the best of their knowledge, skills, or talent. The national anthem calls for national unity. Any sport that calls for the national anthem gains the support of the entire nation. This is natural about the national anthem.

It unites people and connects them to the country. During the systemic racism protests and COVID-19 pandemic leadership failures, the national anthem was the best tool to unite the country. The reason behind this was that the morale of the government was down. As a result, many people suffered injustice, including George Floyd and insurrectionists who are still in jail. When the morale of the leadership of the country goes down, citizens rise with leadership, role, and responsibility. It is the solemn duty of every citizen to respond to injustice with strength, not weakness. Regardless of how President Trump's government disregarded leadership to protect citizens against systemic racism and the COVID-19 pandemic, kneeling during the national anthem is not the last resort.

National anthem as the pride of the nation.

The national anthem does not only unite the country, but also is the pride of the nation. Whenever the national anthem is sung, I don't see people play politics regardless of their political or immigration affiliation in the country. I see everybody in a standing ovation while the national anthem is sung, including Democrats, Republicans, Blacks, Whites, Latinos, Asians, etc., and/or legal or illegal immigrants. It shows how everybody cares about unity in the country. The national anthem does not discriminate against anybody living in the country. But the government does. Whenever the government fails in leadership, people must rise with leadership, role, and responsibility to strengthen the government or reform it through election. One of the dual duties of every citizen is to support the country even if the leadership of the country collapses. When you are kneeling on the national anthem, you have knelt on the pride of the nation. The leadership, role, and responsibility of the country is not only about the President or the government, but you. The President has only one or two terms to lead the country, but your leadership is infinite. Therefore, the President's lack of leadership to intervene in the affairs of citizens calls for your leadership, role, and responsibility. It shows how the nation is united even if the President discriminates against citizens.

Leadership acts on strength, not weakness.

Leadership acts on strength. It does not act on weakness. Leadership does not create mistakes, but they correct them. How do you kneel on the national anthem to correct the behavior of the leadership of the government who failed to intervene in systemic racism and COVID-19 issues? I saw no difference between the President, who disregarded his leadership role and responsibility to intervene in the systemic racism and COVID-19 pandemic issues across the nation, and citizens who did not take leadership but kneel on the national anthem. Because there was no difference between the people kneeling on the national anthem and the President, both acted on weakness.

While one acts on weakness, one must act on strength to resolve the issue. This principle can be understood by examining a portable flashlight using battery. The flashlight system is designed with positive and negative ends just as the battery does. When you insert the battery in the flashlight with the negative and positive ends connected, the light is powered and brighten the environment. This is what leadership, role, and responsibility are about. You do not assume your leadership role and responsibility for weakness. You assume your leadership with strength so that you can balance it with weakness when it comes across the way. Based on this, people who kneeled on the national anthem during President Trump's government to get the government's attention acted on weakness. One thing to know is that there is no perfect government or citizen. However, whenever the government acts on weakness, citizens act on strength to balance things out in their homes and/or in the community. It is the heart of leadership.

Let your leadership model the children.

The failed leadership of the country does not change your leadership role and responsibility to model your child about the values of the country. It is the dual role of the parent, guardian, or educator to model the kids about the values of the national anthem. The country's values include the national anthem. The national anthem calls for national unity. Whenever the national anthem is called, not only the people of the United States rise but also people from other countries rise in support of the nation. This value of the national anthem does not only unify people in the United Staes, but also everybody who supports the country. This includes people from the Western and non-Western worlds. Due to this, parents should not kneel on the national anthem but on a standing ovation. It shows parents' leadership, role, and responsibility in support of the nation. Children watch what parents do. Most often, parents' actions become the inspirational foundation for the child. Parents must speak the values of the country to their children and show them leadership, role, and responsibility as a way of modeling them to the next generation. It's the heart of leadership roles and responsibility.

President Biden's government and failed policy curve in Afghanistan and the borders.

While President Biden's government has been praised for enhancing the US foreign policy, he has failed to curve policy in Afghanistan and the US southern borders. Policy is the backbone of government. Regardless of how the government pursues politics, policy helps citizens understand the direction in which the government is heading with the leadership, role, and responsibility. Failure of government to achieve policy goals is a failure of the government. Due to this failure, the President withdrew from Afghanistan and allowed the US southern borders to flood with an immigration crisis.

Failed Policy Curve in Afghanistan.

While many people believe that the US withdrawal from Afghanistan was a mission accomplished, I believe it was a failed policy curve. How would you feel if the mother of democracy lived in your country for over 20 years and exited without leaving any form of democracy behind? Whether this was a coincidence or accident, the President did not curve policy in Afghanistan. Afghans have no democracy in the country. Lack of democracy, Afghan people are wiped of freedom. They have no voice in government, freedom of speech, freedom of worship, and/or freedom of education. How can you reform government without freedom of speech? How can you connect Afghan society without freedom of worship? How can you liberate Afghan people without freedom of education where both men and women are fully taking part? Based on this, the President not only failed to curve policy but also did not take the leadership role and responsibility to maintain democracy in Afghanistan.

Leadership shines over the nation.

While the US withdrawal does not matter in politics, it does matter in leadership, role, and responsibility. Leadership is like a light. It shines in the dark. When leadership missed the opportunity to shine over the nation, they missed the opportunity to use their leadership role and responsibility as the source of light to shine on the people. They also missed the chance to project light beams from their leadership to clear darkness over people. When leadership is lacking in the community, the people live in the dark. The dual role and responsibility of leadership is not only to project light beams but also to direct the projection of light beams from the light source to light up areas covered in the dark and liberate people. The US withdrawal from Afghanistan showed that the leadership did not project or direct the light beams on the Afghan people. This is how I experienced in President Biden's government. The withdrawal from Afghanistan left Afghans in the dark. It is a failed policy curve. Due to this, President Biden's government does not influence Afghanistan.

Lack of US influence in the Afghan region.

President Biden's government did not only fail to lead Afghans to a successful democracy, but the government did not also keep influence in the Afghan region. Due to this, the political bond between the US and Afghans is broken, leaving a gap between the US and Afghans. This gap has never been filled. The President has not curved policy in Afghanistan. Afghans are yet to battle in the hustle environment: no democracy, no freedom. You cannot imagine the state in which the Taliban government is struggling with democracy, leadership, role, and responsibility. However, you can imagine that the Taliban government has no resources enough to govern the country. Based on this, the US withdrawal did not only end democratic leadership in Afghanistan, but it also did not connect with the Taliban enough to offer support. The absence of US influence in the region caused Afghan people to go back to their original state. However, Afghan heroes are living in exile, the youth are confused, women are deprived of education, Afghans are betrayed in their own country, and the political bond between the US and Afghanistan is broken.

Afghan heroes in exile

The failed policy curve in Afghanistan resulted in Afghan heroes living in exile in the United States. I would think that the people that led to the full birth of democracy in Afghanistan would fight and sustain it, but they flew the country. President Biden flew these heroes out of the country and left the young youth, women, and children vulnerable. How do you define leadership, role, and responsibility? Those heroes who were flown to the United States not only embraced democracy in the country, but they also lived it. They believe all Afghan people are one nation and one leadership at a time and should not see themselves as different. Unfortunately, these people who embraced democracy in Afghanistan now live in exile here in the United States. Was this a coincidence or an accident? I believe that these heroes would not have left Afghanistan if they had the US support. How can you grow democracy if you do not have expects in leadership roles and responsibility? how would you sustain democracy without infrastructure in place? The struggling Afghan government shows that there are no expects on the ground, no infrastructure, and no resources. Based on this, there are no true changes in the Afghan state.

No true change in Afghanistan

Over two decades of the US presents in Afghanistan, I have seen a true change in Afghanistan. I have seen democracy bear roots over the years in the country. I have witnessed Afghans mobilize military battalions across the country. I saw a Democratic president in Afghanistan, free education where both males and females go to school and take part in politics and sports. I saw a successful government that cares for the people. I have seen these changes come to Afghanistan. I believe 100% that the Afghans' trust in Americans was restored. They were motivated and confident to take leadership, role, and responsibility for their country. But they were not ready enough without the US present in Afghanistan. It means that the US hadn't finished its diplomatic engagement with the country by reconciling the government with the Taliban.

Failed Diplomatic engagement

A failed policy curve in Afghanistan led to the failed achievement of diplomatic engagement in the country. There was no mutual departure of the US government in Afghanistan. The withdrawal was a betrayal of the Afghan citizens with the Taliban leadership and destruction of the US relationship with Afghanistan. It did not only affect the Afghan people, but it also affected the US influence in the region. It was a political accident. This political accident has caused damage to the US achievement in Afghanistan.

The US captured Osama Biden Laden, reformed democratic government, and allowed equal education for both men and women in the country. While these achievements yielded a positive change in the country, there were no plans to sustain the government or to support the Taliban to rule the country. Due to this, the Afghan democratic government collapsed to the Taliban. However, there was no mutual relationship between the US and the Taliban government to keep freedom for Afghans. This was a failed diplomatic engagement. How would you collapse the Afghan democratic government and have no mutual ties with the Taliban to keep democracy in the country? Was this a coincidence or an accident? Or a lack of information?

Lack of information resulted in withdrawal

Over twenty years of the US relationship with the Afghan people was enough to leave the country without early withdrawal peacefully. Why? Because the Afghan people had a democratic government to take over. If the government was not ready enough, how did President Biden's government justify withdrawal? Often, leaders do not judge on what they see but on what they find. What did President Biden's government find in the Afghan democratic government to call for withdrawal? If you did not find anything about the readiness of the Afghan democratic government, it means you did not explore enough. In other words, if you explored the sufficient leadership, you would have had enough information to plan the withdrawal.

Information is the hallmark of leadership

As the government, you must engage in exploration and ensure that you have enough information for analysis and decision-making. It will help you to develop plans and update strategies beforehand for a secured withdrawal. Collection of evidence from exploration also provides you with information that is credible to balance your short and long-term goals in leadership. It means that once the President had planned to pull out of Afghanistan, he must complete an investigation to examine the readiness of the Afghan government. The absence of exploration led to the quick withdrawal and collapse of the Afghan democratic government. While the early pullout was not intentional, it lacked enough information to plan out. Due to this, the President not only failed to achieve diplomatic engagement with the Afghan people, but he also failed to help them sustain the government.

Fail policy to sustain the Afghan government

Sustaining the government is as critical as reforming the government. The Afghan government could not stand without mechanisms to maintain itself. The mechanisms to maintain the government include financial, military, partnership, and/or diplomatic mechanisms. When these mechanisms are set up to maintain the government, you dare break them, or else the government will collapse. The sustainability of every government is critical to positively affecting the people. In Afghanistan, I believe these mechanisms were set up for the Afghan government to succeed while the US promoted its interest in the region. Those mechanisms were not set up to be broken any soon. It was set up to ensure free Afghans advance with democracy so that the US footprint is not wiped from the region. The mechanisms were not set up by themselves. People set it up. People sacrificed their lives to set up the mechanisms. What I want to put across here is that the US men and women in uniform reformed the Afghan government and military. It was a nightmare for the US troops and Afghan people because it was all over the world. It means that people lost their lives to reform the government. How will you feel if the sacrifices of the US men and women in Afghanistan are not sustained? However, this is what happened in President Biden's government. The President rushed the withdrawal. It has caused the Afghan people a lasting nightmare.

Nightmares after the US withdrawal

One of the worst nightmares to imagine is the ramifications after the US withdrawal from Afghanistan. The Afghan women are held in bondage at home, and the heroes of Afghan democracy remain in exile. Are these stories still fresh in your mind? They are still fresh in my mind. I have heard stories such as these about the olden days. I have listened to a story about the olden days when women used to manage the kitchen while the men managed the groceries. However, in the modern era, both males and females work and take care of the grocery and kitchen, go to school and share equal leadership in politics. Afghan women do not have this freedom. It was taken away from them. Afghan men and women who embraced democracy as the hallmark of liberty are in exile here in the United States. How would you suggest a policy curve in Afghanistan when Afghan women are less likely to go to school, work, or take part in government? How would you suggest a policy curve in Afghanistan when the Afghan heroes who were trained to grow democracy in the country were taken into exile? If you can engage with the Afghan heroes in a crucial conversation, they will tell you that they are better off in Afghanistan. It is the worst nightmare to imagine about Afghan people at home and Afghan heroes in exile. They are traumatized. They are living with the worst nightmares. It's the ramification of the withdrawal.

Afghans are back to their original state.

The Afghans are back to their original darkness after the US withdrawal. Over twenty years of US presence in Afghanistan, Afghan men and women pursued democracy, but they have never achieved it. They have no democracy, less education for women, and no freedom of speech about injustice in Afghan society. Even as Afghan men and women are born equal, women have less opportunity to pursue education, take public or private jobs, or join politics. How would you feel as an Afghan woman if you were restricted not to going to school, taking public jobs, and being confined at home?

The state of rejecting democracy and depriving women showed the original state of the country. Regardless of politics, no government rejects freedom. The dual role of government is to keep democracy and the rule of law and move the country forward, not backward. However, the US withdrawal led to Afghan democracy moving backward. It has affected the Afghan youth. Afghan youth are confused about the direction of the country.

Confused Afghan youth

The Afghan youth remain confused after the US withdrawal. The youth understand the situation in which they are put in as the result of the withdrawal. However, they had no clue whether the US withdrawal was due to politics or leadership roles and responsibilities. The Afghan youth are now in an imagination about what has happened to their country. The Afghan youth were born in the democratic government of Afghanistan. The youth were born during the time of the United States' presence in the country. So, they were born in freedom, in a democratic leadership of the country. They had no physical intimacy with the past dictatorships of government in the country. The little the youth know about the country is the freedom the US has given to them. The youth embraced freedom as the hallmark of their country.

They experienced democratic leadership in the country, freedom of worship, speech, and education. They experienced both boys and girls going to school together and playing sports across the country. The youth were thankful for the US government's support of the country. They were also grateful for the freedom. These are all what I believe the Afghan youth know about. Can you imagine any? While the youth pursued freedom to the highest level of the country, they were ready to advance it. However the leadership of the government was not prepared to sustain the government. The leadership was desperate for support from the US to sustain the government. This was a call for President Biden's leadership, role, and responsibility to intervene, but the President did not curve the policy. Due to this, the Afghan government collapsed to the Taliban rule without democracy. The confused Afghan youth who pursued freedom to the best of their ability are now stacked in the mud of dictatorship, which they had never experienced. It is why the Afghan youth live humiliated.

The humiliated Afghan youth

The Afghan youth were not only confused about the US withdrawal but they were also humiliated. If you can imagine the level of humiliation that the Afghan youth went through after the withdrawal, you would understand that the withdrawal was torture to them. I will bet that the Afghan youth were disappointed because the US could not help them sustain freedom in the country. How can you agree that the mother of democracy left Afghanistan without leaving any form of democracy behind? Was this a coincidence or an accident? While the US pullout makes sense in politics, it does not make sense in leadership, role, and responsibility. Due to this, President Biden did not curve policy in Afghanistan.

As a result, the Afghan democratic government collapsed. Whatever happened between President Biden and the Afghan democratic leader did not curve policy in Afghanistan. The Afghan youth were caught up in the middle of failed leadership and policies to sustain democracy and government. The youth were frustrated and humiliated because they could not handle the political stress of being discriminated against in their own country. Women were not given equal opportunities as men to go to school and join politics. These Afghan youth were naturally transformed by the freedom of education provided by the US. It was just a matter of time before the youth could step into leadership roles and responsibility to liberate the country. However, this privilege was taken away from them on the day of withdrawal. This is how I viewed it. What about you?

Rejection of Afghan youth

Was the US withdrawal from Afghanistan a sign of rejecting the Afghan youth? The withdrawal of the US troops from Afghanistan was not enough to justify the rejection of the Afghan youth. However, it was sufficient to justify that President Biden did not curve policy in Afghanistan. The policy does not drive itself. Leadership roles and responsibility drive policy. The failed leadership role and responsibility of the President led to a failed policy curve in Afghanistan, the collapse of the Afghan democratic government, and leaving Afghan youth confused, frustrated, and humiliated. It is fair to say that the US does not reject Afghan youth. Afghan youth are always welcome in the United States in the pursuit of democracy. The Afghan child, whether Taliban or not Taliban, is welcome because the US does not discriminate against people pursuing democracy. Based on this argument, I believe that the US is the mother of democracy and has a leadership role and responsibility to welcome people who seek democracy.

Even as the US leadership failed to curve policy in Afghanistan, Afghan youth has a leadership role and responsibility to reengage with the US for freedom. Once freedom is born in Afghanistan, Afghan youth have the choice to grow it or kill it. The US withdrawal does not prevent the Afghan leadership from reengaging with the US. Even as the US is gone, Afghans have a lasting relationship with the US leadership. Therefore, the Taliban government can reach out to the US leadership for help to liberate the youth with freedom. In this way, the Afghan youth will not lack the privilege they need to pursue democracy.

The betrayed Afghans

The US's quick withdrawal from Afghanistan left many Afghans betrayed in their own country. I would imagine that the Afghans could not trust each other. The new leadership could not trust the people because the new government was not sure if the US withdrawal was a setup. Also, it was shocking to believe that the Afghan governing military would lose their guide. Based on this, the Taliban leadership sees some Afghans as a threat because they share different views. Due to this, the Taliban will not give many Afghans the opportunity to pursue democracy in the country. This holdback was due to President Biden's unplanned withdrawal from the country. Over the past two decades of the US presence in Afghanistan, many Afghans embraced democracy as the hallmark of their culture. They wake up every day and feel connected with the community and government. They go to school, secure private or public jobs, and take care of their homes and communities. They cast votes to elect public leaders of the country. Afghans were used to democratic culture. Culture of freedom – the culture that embraced women's rights to education and politics. While this new democratic culture gave birth to a new vision for the Afghan youth, President Biden collapsed it.

Born ally of the United States.

Afghan people are born allies of the United States, whether Taliban or non-Taliban. Over two decades of democratic rule in Afghanistan, Afghan youth have been inspired to pursue democracy in the country through elections. Even though the Taliban government has been in the US for over two decades, they understand that the people embraced democracy as the hallmark of the country. The youth enjoyed freedom. Both men and women went to school and joined politics, and elections were held, and the President was elected. However, the US withdrawal gave the Taliban government two options: to pursue democracy or dictatorship. Whichever way is sooner, the country is a born ally of the US. The US withdrawal from Afghanistan does not prevent the Afghan government from connecting with the US for support to liberate the youth. The current chaotic situation in Afghanistan shows that the Taliban were not prepared to take over the government. They were prepared to work side by side with the Afghan democratic government. However, President Biden's failed policy curve led to the Taliban forming the government. While you think the President is building allies, he is breaking them. The President has broken the political born between the US and Afghanistan.

Broken political bond

The US withdrawal ends the US relationship with the Afghans. Once there is no relationship in the country, there is no influence in the region. The withdrawal has broken the political bond between the two countries. I would think that over twenty years of the US relationship with the Afghans, President Biden will keep a long-term political relationship with them. However, the President did not plan for any relationship with the country. Therefore, there was no mutual plan to hand power to the Taliban. He abandoned it. Due to this fragmentation of politics, the President broke the political bond between the two countries. Today, the relationship sours. It has become very dangerous to reengage in the relationship. While the US can repair the US-Afghan political bond, it is extremely dangerous and expensive to reengage with the Afghan people. It is not too late, but it is too soon to repair the relationship. Because there are no elements of trust for re-engagement in the relationship, the Afghan people are more desperate than before, having lost their fundamental rights to freedom. It shows how leadership did not assume its leadership role and responsibility.

Nevertheless, the Taliban government will find its way to unit with the US government. In this way, the Taliban would bring all Afghans together to form a democratic government. Thus, I believe the Afghans will find a new way of freedom as they hope to reengage with the US in the future.

Afghan parents before the withdrawal

Before the US withdrawal, Afghan parents developed a new family relationship with themselves, their children, and the community. Husband and wife both understood the freedom to individually take outside jobs, work, and bring money home to support the family. They also understand that two paychecks boost the family's income and help them take care of the kids. When parents have enough money at home, they can plan for the family. They can start thinking about life beyond their home. They can think about vacations and travel across other countries. They also think big about the future of their country and their children. They would send their children to school and have them complete college. They will start planning better things about their daughters than just confining them to their homes. They understand that their daughters are as equal to their sons in every aspect, including leadership roles and responsibility.

This is what happened to many Afghan parents who pursued freedom at the highest level of parenting. Parents were motivated to engage with their kids and talk to them about freedom and good family relationships.

Empowered Afghan female

The US presence in Afghanistan not only helped Afghans enhance their family relationships but it also helped them empower the female population across the country. Families begin to nurture young girls about the freedom to go to school, learn, and become leaders of the country. They have made the young females understand that they are as equal as males. The young girls know that they can do whatever the male does. The young Afghan girls were motivated. They were happy to go to school and learn side by side with their male counterparts. The girls had their minds set on making a difference in education and advancing their careers in politics and government.

This shows how Afghan women embraced education. This new culture of women to go to school, work, and get involved in government seized after the US withdrawal. Looking at the progress the Afghan women have achieved, they did not deserve the dictatorship of the country today. Afghan women live in captivity

There is nothing to think about President Biden's quick withdrawal from Afghanistan than to imagine how the Afghan women live in captivity as a result of the withdrawal. The withdrawal wiped democracy in Afghanistan and put women in captivity. Women in Afghanistan are discriminated against academically, socially, and politically. You don't need to think too much to understand the situation. Just imagine it. The Taliban leadership will not allow the female freedom to go to school, work outside of their homes take public jobs, and/or take part in politics. This sounds like the female is held captive. Usually, people in captivity have no choice but to do what they are told. They are compelled to remain compliant or face sanctions. They are given the same clothes and bedding, and are told what to eat for breakfast, lunch, and dinner. People in captivity have less privilege to offer any opinion to the authorities about their needs and concerns. This is the situation I see the female Afghans after the US pullout of the country. The Afghan female rights are limited. They have less influence to convince the government about their rights to pursue education, jobs, and politics. The worst of all is that their cry cannot be heard here in the US.

Failed immigration policy curve at the US Southern borders.

President Biden's failed policy curve in Afghanistan also led to a failed immigration policy curve at the US southern borders. What is happening at the US Southern borders? Over the decades, the immigration policy at the US southern borders has become a troubling nightmare. People are killed, arrested, and/or incarcerated. What you see at the US border today did not happen today. Immigrants flow from the South to North America to settle with their families.

It is not a new story. It's an ongoing border challenge that every leadership here in America faces. Many leaders have tried different approaches, yet the situation at the border is worsening. Regardless of the difficulties, every leader has various strategies to control the border. It means that the immigration policies at the border are not static. It is dynamic. However, none of the US leaders have asked the immigrants from the South why they immigrated from the South to the North. This has become the gap that is never filled. Until the US leadership interviews the immigrants and gets to understand why they come to the border, the gap will not be filled. Therefore, nobody will understand the immigrants.

In this case, immigrants will be misjudged and mistreated at the border not only because the US leadership does not understand them but also because the border immigration policy does not meet the standards of managing modern immigrants at the border. Therefore, the current border immigration policy does not meet the intended purpose. If the decades of immigration policies are not helping resolve the border crisis, why is that still enforced? The best way to meet modern immigrants' needs at the southern borders is to develop modern policies.

Develop modern policies for modern immigrants.

The current US immigration policy at the southern borders does not serve the intended purpose. When policy does not serve its intended purpose, it damages them. It is causing people to lose their lives, arrested, and/or incarcerated. Why should people lose their lives, be arrested, or be detained at the border because they are trying to earn a living? It is alarming. It is a call for leadership, role, and responsibility to amend the policies to meet the modern border standards. The current border immigration policies must be amended, suspended, put to an end, or get rid of it. You don't have to spend a single second thinking about what to do about it. Develop a new set of border immigration policies that can help balance the needs of modern immigrants at the borders. The current border policy is long too old to resolve the current border crisis. I would think that such immigration policies were good only in the past decades. As time passes, immigration culture changes. New generation, new policy, and new culture. Amend the existing policies. It is not wrong to amend policies and embrace new culture at the borders without arrest, incarceration, or death. Policy is dynamic. It is not static. Therefore, enhancing the southern border immigration policies will not only save its intended purposes but it will help bridge the immigrant gap at the border.

Wipe out old border immigration policies.

Pursuing immigration policies that haven't worked for decades is like chasing the wind (John 3:8). Running around but catching nothing. How do you catch the wind if you cannot see it or even hold it? The wind blows wherever it goes. Wind is not a physical element. It is a spiritual element. You cannot see it, touch it, hold it, or stop it. But you can tell how you feel about it and/or the direction in which it blows. To prevent the wind is to stop the source supplying the wind. If you cannot stop the source from supplying the wind, then you don't get to stop the wind from flowing across your community. This is how I see the immigration situation at the US border with the South.

What is happening physically at the southern border is beyond the border. Regardless of how much time the border patrol officers invest at the border, immigrants will still flow across the border. This is not a new problem. It is an ongoing problem that leaders in America have faced. They have tried to stop immigrants from crossing the border using the border immigration policies that were dead many decades ago. Any border immigration policies that exist now should be wiped off so that new ones are developed. New policies that are conducive for the country and immigrants at the border. This should not be the Democrats or Republicans, but the Congressmen and women and all Americans.

Plan beyond the border

When you limit border immigration policies to the border, you have limited vision beyond the border. It is not about the open-door policies that trap immigrants at the border or increase the number of Border Patrol officers just to have people arrested, incarcerated, or killed at the border. But it is about meeting the needs of the immigrants beyond the border where they came from. It is not wrong to ask immigrants about what they need at the border. As an immigrant, I understand what they need. They need a better future for their families. They need jobs, safety, and security.

These are the stories I hear from my friends who immigrated through the southern borders. Southern countries are struggling with economic depressions and safety and security issues. No jobs. They live in a troubling nightmare every day. I also hear stories from my immigrant friends that the entire South American Region lacks regional unity, collaboration, and resources to fight safety and security issues and create jobs for the people. If this is the case, how can leadership help bridge these gaps? How can you help immigrants crossing the border avoid being arrested, incarcerated, or struggling somewhere around the border and being killed? How can the leadership of North and South America find a common ground to help meet immigrant needs?

Developing regional collaboration

Help create the North-South American Regional Collaboration Task Force (NSRCTF) to manage the security, safety, and job issues in the region. Without this, living at the border will continue to be eminent. People will desperately travel to the border, feel unfortunate, get humiliated, and die without purpose. How soon can leadership enhance the security, safety, and job issues affecting the region and help the vulnerable population find jobs, settle with family, and avoid being arrested, incarcerated, or killed as a result of traveling through dangerous routes?

How can you shelter people without a structure? In other words, without a structure, how can you shelter people? Without a regional entity to address the safety, security, and job issues that matter to immigrants, people will travel in a harmful way to the border. Regional collaboration is required to develop short and long-term strategic plans that will support the safety, security, and job issues affecting the regional population. Therefore, dialogue is critical in the region. With dialogue, the US can direct resources spent at the border to support the regional initiatives. The North-south regional collaboration is critical to ensure the safety, security, job, and orderly flow of immigrants in the region. This will help people from being arrested, incarcerated, or killed at the border.

Enhance leadership roles and responsibilities at the border.

The failed leadership role and responsibility to develop a new border policy led to immigrants crossing the US southern borders facing an imminent threat. They are facing life-and-death situations. When you put the shoes of those parents carrying their babies at the back while walking through the wild to the border, you will see a failed leadership role and responsibility to meet the needs of people. Nobody cares how these people are fed or survive during the entire journey. It makes the situation so troubling because there are thousands of people fleeing through the border every year in the same dangerous situation. How do you blame these people if there are issues with policy and leadership to direct them? Leadership failed not only these people at their homes but also at the border. Therefore, leadership fails them wherever they go. Is this a coincidence or an accident? The question is, how soon are leaderships across these jurisdictions working to bridge this gap? How do you define leadership, role, and responsibility in the border immigration crisis?

Help me, or do not worsen my problem.

My dad used to say, "If you cannot help me carry down the load from my head, do not add any more load to it." In other words, if you cannot help resolve my case, do not make it worse. The immigrant cases at the US Southern Border are the worst. They are not only dying in the wild, but they are also arrested, incarcerated, or separated from their loved ones. If you cannot help these people at the border who are looking for a better future, why have them arrested, incarcerated, or spend time in the jungle and get killed by the wild? If you cannot help them, let them find their way out. It makes an enormous difference when that happens.

It is not about them. It's about the policy and leadership role and responsibility at the border and beyond the border. What would you do if you did not have a job to take care of your family? You would need to find a job. These people are looking for jobs. You can give them a job or create one for them. They are not selective. They are ready to do any job. They met all labor requirements for any job, but leadership must act on policy and direct them to the resources. It's the dual role and responsibility of leadership to create jobs and engage people to work. Instead of leadership engaging people with work, leadership is arresting people and incarcerating them, not only depriving them of work but also disabling their hope and vision to live better. It is a fundamentally failed policy.

Policy as dialogue

Policy is a dialogue and must be clear enough for people to understand, interpret, and communicate it at all levels at the border. This is how policy speaks to people. If I do not understand your policy, it is not clear enough, and I cannot interpret it well the way you want it. Due to this, I would not get the directions I need to navigate through the business as you need me. This is the situation I experienced at the US Southern Borders. The border immigration policy is not clear enough for immigrants to understand, interpret, and communicate it. Immigrants interpret it the way they know it, just to come to the border and be arrested, incarcerated, and/or killed. It is not about the people. It is about the policy. Policy bounces when not understood by the public.

Policy becomes a bouncing element in society if not clear enough to understand, interpret, and communicate. It bounces back and forth in society until leadership takes its leadership role and responsibility to fix it. This means that people will always reject policies that they do not understand. However, leadership has a role and responsibility to develop policies that work for people and help them individually or collectively, not only to know and understand such policies but also to be able to communicate them.

The way you communicate the policy to the immigrants shows how they understand it. When you communicate it well, they will understand it well. When you do not communicate the policy well to the public, it bounces back to you. People are going to reject it not only because they do not understand it but also because they do not know how to use it. Leadership must invest time and resources to engage research experts in the field to conduct research and produce the best approach to deal with border policies and immigration at the southern borders. It will help reduce the follow of immigrants at the border.

Help immigrants understand the policy.

If I can come to the border and cross it, I will make my way to the border. It is not how well you enforce policy but how well you communicate it. It is often a two-way street where leaders and immigrants can meet in the middle of the policy to achieve the goal of the policy. It is how many organizations that deliver services are highly effective because they are communicating well with their audiences: clients or customers. For example, when you go shopping in the store, you need store representatives who are ready not only to welcome you to the store but also to help you get the things that you are looking for in the store.

The more the store representatives help you with your needs, the more you develop a bond with the store and love to shop in the store. This is how many people behave when they go shopping in the store. They need people who understand the business and services and can help explain to them. They do not need attitude. When expected to understand the business and services, step up, and offer help, it changes the atmosphere of the client or customer. They will not spend time wandering in the store. It is how you can communicate policy to audiences. It is not only about what your policy says about customer service but also about how your staff understands your policy, accepts the culture of the environment, and is willing to stay engaged with the audience. It is how the staff takes leadership, role, and responsibility of the business to the highest level of the company's policies. This principle also works for managing immigration policies at the border. Every level of leadership must understand the immigration policy as they communicate to the immigrants because policy reflects the culture at the border.

Policy as a blueprint

The tension about the fragmented policy across the US Southern borders helps us understand that policy is not only a dialogue but also a blueprint of a construction project that helps engineers understand the project before they start it. I would imagine how the layperson would understand an engineering project without a complete blueprint of the project. The blueprint is the map of the project from start to finish. So, understanding the blueprint will help you understand the spectrum of the project. This is the same concept as understanding the policy at the border or in any organization. The policy at the border is public and changes whenever a new government is formed. Politicians often announce their intentions during the campaign trails across the country through the media. This means that everybody understands how the border policy is executed at the border beforehand, or everybody knows what the border policy is going to look like in a new regime. Whatever politicians advocated during the campaign is what they are going to do when they form the government.

However, it is tough to imagine how policies are fragmented at the border because politicians do not always do as said. Why? Policy sounds good when you speak it, but most often, when you implement policy, it does not always appear the way you spoke it. Policy works well after the implementation only when you have experts onboard to carry it on the way it was said. Obviously, experts will make it sound even better because they understand it and care to be advocates of the policy. The experts will not mislead the public, because they understand the policy as the blueprint and freely communicate it to the public. However, the tension at the US southern borders shows that the border policy was not well implemented.

Engage policy experts at the border.

Policy is not politics. Engage policy experts to study the border. Construction managers and engineers interpret construction blueprints, so policy experts develop and interpret policies. Only people who understand construction blueprints can interpret it very well on the ground. Blueprint is given to a person who understands it, not a person who cannot interpret it. When you design a blueprint for your construction project, you don't give it to the lawyer; you give it to the construction manager or engineer. The engineer will ensure that your blueprint project is conducted exactly as designed.

The engineer will transfer dimensions from the blueprint to the ground. The engineer will not only ensure the exact delivery of the project but also ensure the quality and artistry of the project. It is how experts do in the field. Not every politician can interpret every policy. Politicians are experts in speculating on policies to help policy experts draft policies that resonate with people.

People who advocate policy must ensure that they understand and address policy in the simplest terms for society to understand. If you do not advocate policy well, you are going to confuse people. This is what happened at the US southern borders. People are confused about whether the government is building a wall or allowing the open-door policy. The more people understand where you stand in your policy, the better you are at achieving the goals. If the government cannot make the border immigration policy clear to the public, then the border will be crowded with immigrants. Immigrants at the border will continue to be arrested and incarcerated. It is not fair for the immigrants.

The role of business organizations in the country.

What confused American politicians in Washington was also confusing to the public, who thought that Amazon, Facebook, Twitter, or Google business organizations were wrong in their intervention on the January 6 insurrection. The leadership of business organizations is not only supplying services to the American public but also serving the people and country in that role. Once these organizations do business with the American people, they have a leadership role and responsibility to protect the American people, businesses, and the country against threats. It is part of their service to the country. It shows not only their leadership role and responsibility but also the integrity of the business organization. It also shows respect and care to the clients or customers who do business with the organization. It helps assess the level of leadership role and responsibility of the organization to run the business safely and securely for the American public. Therefore, the leaders of Amazon, Facebook, Twitter, and Google business organizations understand that their business is not only about the organization but also about the people, community, and the nation.

Business organizations as first responders

Business organizations across the country, regardless of how big or small, are not only supplying services to the people but are also the first respondents of the country against threat. On the January 6 insurrection, the leadership of Twitter, Amazon, Facebook, and Google acted in their abilities to ensure the safety and security of the country and the people they serve. The organizations did not only support the country by such an intervention, ensuring safety and security but also protecting the integrity of the country. This is not political. It is duty. It is usual for enemies from abroad to attack the country. Still, it is not usual when the government of the country and citizens are involved in attacks against the country where people are killed and property is destroyed. The actions of Twitter, Amazon, Apple, and Google show the kind of leadership that I am presenting to you and your family, as well as business here in America. It is not political but duty. It is the duty of all organizations' leaders, private or public, profit or nonprofit, large or small, to respond to any threat that comes against the country directly or indirectly from their area of business. HHA. Your help in supporting the country is as important as everybody else supporting the nation. It is the heart of leadership, role, and responsibility.

Leadership as the light of the business

The leadership of every organization is not only part of the first respondents of the country but also the light of the business as well as the country. The organizers' leadership light shines over the business and attracts people to partner with the organization. Without the lights of leadership, business will be in the dark, and people will not see it. When leadership switches off the lights in the organization, the business will be gone. The environment will not only be dark and blurry for people to navigate through the organization, but the atmosphere will also not be conducive to business. I would agree that the leadership of Amazon, Apple, Twitter, Facebook, and Google might have good reasons to justify their intervention in the January 6 insurrection. Their leadership, to me, shows that they are lights not only for business but also for the nation and everybody who partners with them. Not only did they fulfill their duty as professionals in business, but they also fulfilled the obligation to protect the country as citizens.

No organization is limited to safety and security interventions of the country.

There is not any organization that is limited from safety and security interventions to protect the business and the community that they serve. The action of Amazon, Apple, Twitter, and Google on the January 6 insurrection tells every American not only to think of the military and police as the first respondence to public threat but also themselves. Leadership does not single anybody out of leadership, role, and responsibility to protect the country, community, and home that they live in.

How many times has somebody told you to mow the lawn of your home before you mow it? Or how many times has someone told you to clean your home before you clean it? The same way you would mow the lawn of your home, keep it clean, safe, and secure for your family, is the same way you are responsible for mowing the lawn of the country. It is the call of leadership. I believe that we all have a responsibility to protect the country just as we do ourselves: homes, communities, and businesses. There is not a single person across the country who is limited by what she or he can do to protect the community or country against threat or insurrection. Everybody is an ordained leader growing up in the family and is shaped by parents or guardians, the culture of the community, and the country. Regardless of how your life is shaped, the integrity of your home, community, and country is not a tampering rag, and you must judiciously protect it. It's a call for your leadership role and responsibility.

How leadership light shines at home.

Leadership is light and shines for society. It shines from your home community and goes across the country. The leadership of parents or guardians is at home. It shines across the floors, hallways, stairways, and the rooms. The lights help the entire family walk through everywhere in their home without stumbling because they can see everything, everywhere in their home. The lights help them partner with the kitchen to prepare food for breakfast, lunch, and dinner. The lights can also help the family see the dirt in their home, remove the dirt, and brighten the environment of their home. Besides this, the leadership of parents lights the home and makes the home a conducive place to live. When parents keep their leadership lights on at home, it will eventually brighten not only the interior of the home but also the exterior. It will attract neighbors, friends, and people in the community and help engage them to collectively build the community. Just as lights shine indiscriminately, so does leadership in society.

Leadership creates a safe environment for people.

Leadership does not only shine for society but also creates a safe environment for their people. Leadership brings light to people, secures boundaries, and masks homes, communities, and the country against vulnerabilities. Leadership supplies people with the lens to visualize the internal and external environment of their homes. It helps people assess the safety and security level outside before they walk out of their homes. Once leadership supplies a lens, you do not walk in the community with the assumption of what is going on, but you walk with clarity in your conscience because you can see everything through your leadership. Your leadership does not depend on politics or the news media for information on how to lead your people. Politics does not decide how you take care of your people, but your leadership. Leadership is light, so you can see the spectrum of your government, have full control of your leadership, and ensure that collaboration within your leadership team is adequate. Leadership always has a resource lineup to resolve problems. Once your leadership is light, you can see the big picture of your environment the opportunities, threats, and challenges to overcome them.

There is no dignity in society without leadership.

There is no dignity in society without leadership. Without leadership, the world will be a cold, dark, wild, and scary place to live. In other words, there will be no law, order, or dignity in our society. Leadership is light. Without leadership, there is no light in our society. Light not only makes society a beautiful and conducive place, but it also encourages people to work in the field because they can see everywhere in the environment. I cannot imagine how I can live in my home without light because home is about light. Light makes transforms a home into a better home. Because light at home makes you and your family turn on the air conditioner to cool yourselves or turn on the heat to warm yourselves in the winter, it also helps you and your family to cook, enjoy music, and shout for joy. When there is no light in your home, community, and in your country, the entire environment will be cold, dark, wild, and a scary place to live. It is how critical leadership is in our society. Leadership makes everything possible for people. Leadership does not feed people in their homes, but it gives people the opportunity to work hard and help themselves. Due to the inevitable role and responsibility of leadership in our society, everybody must accept leadership as something that we nurture, develop, and practice not only to brighten ourselves, our homes, communities, or the country but also to protect them. If we don't protect our country, homes, and communities, we are most likely to lose our freedom and live in a jungle.

Serve as a role model in your leadership. Avoid serving the devil in you.

Now that you have the power as a gift of the universe, who are you going to serve? Are you going to serve the angel in you or the devil? The choice you make here defines your personality in society. When you choose to serve the devil in you, your whole being sours in the community. This is where many people fail in their leadership roles and responsibility. Many people chose to serve the devil in them. Due to this, their leadership role and responsibility sours in the society. Even as they are chosen to liberate people, they are liberating themselves since their self-egos overshadow their ambition to shine over people. Nobody is destined to serve the devil. If you are serving the devil, you are serving the mysterious world where leadership roles and responsibility are defined as fulfilling personal desires. Regardless of how long you keep the powers of your God-given, your leadership role and responsibility sours. Nothing concerns you about the community. But the community is the heart of your leadership role and responsibility. When you lose the community, you don't have a home. But when you lose your home, you can always live in the community. You are destined to lead not only your home but also your community. Balance your leadership role and responsibility and shine over the entire area of your leadership. It's what you are destined to do.

Serve your inner angel.

Now that you have the power as the gift of the universe, you are destined to serve the angel in you because you are the light of society. When you shine from the inside out, you are projecting light beams from yourself to your home and community. In this way, you are helping people to walk out of the dark from their homes and community to the light. This is what you are destined to do. Assume your leadership role and responsibility not only to serve your home and community but also to shine over them and model the people. Your affiliation with your home and community is not political but destiny. When you serve the angel in you, you are pursuing your destiny calls. You are called to serve not only as a role model in your leadership role and responsibility but also in your home, community, and in your business. This is what you are destined to do. You can choose to serve the devil, but you are destined to shine over society. Therefore, pursue your role as a leader and assume your leadership role and responsibility as a parent, guardian, businesswoman or man, educator, law enforcement officer, Judge, or whoever you are as a person. When you acknowledge yourself as the light of society, it helps you to understand that you have a duty to project this light to your society. You have a duty not to hold this light and keep your people in the dark. As usual, you don't want to miss the opportunity to liberate your home and community. In other words, you do not want to regret it at the last minute when you don't have the opportunity to liberate your people with your leadership role and responsibility.

Leadership and entitlement as a citizen

Leadership is not about the position, but it is about the person. Your entitlement as an American is a permanent pride that must drive your aspirations to model yourself and the people around you to develop a positive mindset for the nation. It drives your aspirations and everybody living in the United States to model themselves collectively or individually with leadership, role, and responsibility to serve the country right from where they are. You could serve the country from your home or community. When you shine over your home and community, you can shine across the nation. While you live this entitlement, you have an obligation to positively work together with other people and shield the country that you cherish with a vote, not insurrection. It means that the failure of the country's leadership does not change your perspective on positively leading your people at the front.

However, it enhances your awareness about the kind of leadership that should be encouraged in public offices. It is not about the party. But it is about the leadership leading the country. You can be a Democrat, Republican, or Independent, but your leadership, role, and responsibility for the country have not changed. You have the entitlement of being American. Whether you are a citizen or noncitizen, immigrant or non-immigrant, Christian or Muslim, once you live in America, you have the entitlement of the United States to model yourself and fit the culture of the country. In other words, your home is where you live, not where you came from. It's the heart of leadership roles and responsibility. Your leadership accounts for a safe and secure community. Regardless of how old or young you are, you have the entitlement as a citizen to serve the country from where you live, work, or do business. You are affiliated with the country as much as you are affiliated with your home, job, and business.

Serve the country from your home.

Serving the country from your home means you are serving the country from where you live. Your leadership, role, and responsibility in your home show how you serve the country. In your home, you care for everybody in your family. It shows how you serve your home with leadership, role, and responsibility. You ensure that you are giving everybody in your family the opportunity to work hard and help themselves. You also give them the leadership light to see the opportunity to explore and discover their potential. It shows that you care for your home and family. In this way, you have claimed entitlement to your home and family. Because you love your home and family, it's where you live and cherish. You are always ensuring that your home is secured. Every day, when you are leaving your home, you ensure that the doors are locked and cameras are active. You also ensure that the environment is safe before you leave your home.

There is nothing personal about you leaving your home safe and secure. You just don't want intruders to penetrate your home. Due to this, many homes are secured by surveillance cameras. Because people want to know what is happening in their homes while they are away, it's cool when you know that your home is well-equipped with security measures. Because your home is where you live, you do not give your home away, or you will not have a place to live.

This is the mindset that draws your attention to secure your home. It's the same way when you draw your attention to think about the security of the community. When your community is not secured, you are most likely in danger of losing your home. When you lose your community, you will lose your home. But when you lose your home, you can live in the community. Your community is the country where we all live, but your home is your political party. It's critical to shield your country

the same way you shielded your home. Shield the country as you shield your home.

The way you shielded your home is the same way you shielded the country. You shield your home because you love it, care about it, and do not want to lose it. The same way you love the country, care about it and do not want to lose it to enemies. Unfortunately, you have 100% privilege for your home but 25% for the community. It means that you have more responsibility for your home than the community. However, you have the authority to partner with people in the community to decide the leadership of the community to secure the community the same way you secure your home. While the political party candidates are campaigning for power in the country, you have the authority to decide in the ballot the political candidate who is best suited across the country to shield the country as you shield your home.

Political parties often handpick candidates who have more influence to win elections, not candidates who can lead the country. However, the leadership of the country goes beyond a political party. The leadership of the country focuses on the interests of the country as well as the political party. Therefore, screening for political candidates is critical to ensure that the candidate understands the difference between a home and a community. This candidate must understand the ideals of the country, leadership, role, and responsibility. Also, the candidate must understand that the country is not a home or a property but a community. A political party is a home, while the country is a community. You can always sell your home, but you cannot sell the community. If you give your vote to any candidate who thinks the country is home, you will be surprised that this candidate pursues the goals of a single-family home and abandons the security of the community. Your positive reaction and response to things that affect your home and community shows your leadership, role, and responsibility for the country. Just as your voice is critical to managing your family affairs, so your voice is critical to managing the affairs of the country.

Serving the country at your job

The way you shield your job is the same way you shield the country. Many people have used the culture of their work environment to shape their leadership, role, and responsibility in the country. Your affiliation with your work is like your affiliation with your home and community. When you secure a job, you claim the entitlement of the business. In most organizations, the employees are entitled to wear an apron, T-shirt, or jacket with the company's logo on it while they work. It is the entitlement. You have not only become part of the company, but you have also become the company. It means you have reached the entitlement of the business, so you are the business. Whatever services the company administers, you are ready to administer. You serve the company's clients or customers to the best of your ability. Regardless of your status, you are serving the business according to your capacity. Without you, the company will not reach its potential. The company's advancement rests on you. The company's future rests on you. When you show leadership, role, and responsibility in your duty, you will take the company to the next level of its potential. It's the same principles the hospital Nurses applied during the Covid-19 pandemic.

Serving the country as a Nurse

During the Covid-19 pandemic, hospital nurses served the country in the patient bed area. The Nurses understood their leadership role and responsibility to serve the hospitals and medical facilities across the country by making sure that patients get the care they deserve. The nurses not only showed leadership in the nursing profession but also leadership, role, and responsibility by ensuring that every COVID or non-COVID patient in the hospital bed receives care with dignity and respect. Nurses stayed on course. Nurses stood side by side with patients at bedside both day and night, seven days a week. Nurses worked extended hours to ensure that patients received the coverage they needed in the care facilities. Regardless of how COVID-19 separated patients from their families in the hospitals, the hospital nurses were right at patients' bedside, bridging the gaps between patients and families. Regardless of how deadly COVID was, nurses did not quit their jobs, they did not freak out, and they did not complain about the hardship of having patients die in their hands without their families. I feel the nurses served the country with honor. It shows how the hospital nurses seriously took their leadership roles and responsibilities to the highest level of their profession.

Nurses serve patients without political affection.

The hospital Nurses served patients regardless of whether the patients were Democrat, Republican, or Independent. It is the heart of leadership, role, and responsibility. Hospital Nurses understand that they are destined to help patients. It doesn't matter what kind of patient or people. Black or White, or immigrant or non-immigrant. They ensure that every patient gets the best service they deserve. Hospital nurses do not do politics not because they are nurses but because they understand the principles of leadership, role, and responsibility of their job. They have no time for politics. They put parties behind them so that they can take diligent care of patients who come before them. In other words, hospital nurses do not practice personal stuff in the hospital or in their work areas. The patients can play politics by deciding who should take care of them in the hospital. But it is naïve for a patient to do so. The way hospital nurses go the extra mile to take care of every person shows that they understand leadership roles and responsibility. This shows how they work for the country. They do not need to go to the White House to save the country. But they serve the country right from where they work.

The Emergency Medical Services (EMS) personnel

If you can count on the hospital nurses for their outstanding leadership, role, and responsibility during the COVID-19 pandemic, you can also count on the Emergency Medical Services (EMS) personnel across the country. Whether fire or police-linked services, charity ambulances, private, government, and/or Hospitals, or joint emergency services, nobody can deny the sacrifice of the EMS personnel and how they responded to emergency calls during the COVID pandemic. The EMS personnel took leadership, role, and responsibility to the highest level of the job. Every one of them worked not only at a job, but they were passionate about helping save people's lives. It shows leadership in their profession. They understand the principles of leadership, role, and responsibility. When you show leadership at your work, you are not only helping bring change to your company but also helping the country. The way EMS people went door to door, picking up the sick from across the communities and transporting them to the hospital for treatment, was the heart of leadership. It shows how they work for the country. They not only focused on the job but also on the mission to save people who were desperate in their homes.

The efforts of Nurses and EMS personnel

The effort of the hospital nurses and EMS personnel to help sick people is the heart of the leadership role and responsibility. None of these sick people that they are helping are their family members. However, they know and understand that leadership does not discriminate against the people that they serve. They understand that leadership does what matters for the people under their care. They know that they are serving society when they are called into leadership. You are called to serve, and it does not matter what kind of leadership you are called into. You have an obligation to show leadership, role, and responsibility.

It is what the Nurses and EMS personnel did when they were called to serve people during the pandemic. They answered the leadership call and went to work. Most of these Nurses and EMS personnel worked in harm's way. They stood side by side with the patients in the hospital rooms. The Nurses spend the entire time with the patients at the bedside, giving them the necessary care they deserve, while the EMS personnel go door to door carrying the sick and transporting them to the clinics and hospitals. This perspective of the Nurses and EMS personnel indicates how they showed leadership, role, and responsibility at work.

Leadership, Nurses, and EMS personnel.

Nurses and EMS personnel understand the principles of leadership, role, and responsibility in their workplaces. They understand that work is a sacrificial job. If you do not sacrifice enough, you don't get to do enough. But every effort at the workplace goes with leadership, role, and responsibility to ensure that it positively affects society. You know and understand that regardless of how much effort you put in at work, you still need to show leadership, role, and responsibility to affect society. This is what the Nurses and EMS personnel did during the covid. During COVID-19, the EMS personnel and the nurses used their work protocol by wearing masks, washing their hands, and socially distancing themselves while taking care of patients. None of them complained about the challenges of wearing a mask and following social distancing or washing their hands every time. Because they understand that those things must be done before they can do anything to help the sick, it shows how they care for the work they do, the people they serve, and the community they love.

Leadership as the light of the society

Leadership is the light of society. Without leadership, the world will be a dark, wild, and scary place to live. Leadership brings light to people. Leadership masks the nation, spears through boundaries, creates opportunities, and helps people walk out of the darkness into the light. When you have light, your world is bright and shiny because you are not only safe and secure, but also you have met all your basic needs. Your fear will be gone because your home will be decorated with light to help you see all the resources around you. You will have the opportunity to work and support your family. When you have light in your home, you do not worry about crawling creatures. You are going to see them before they get to you, and this is why light is strength. So, as light is strength, leadership is also strength. While you are leading your family, community, and your country, you are shining over your family, community, and the country.

Leadership as light in your home

Your leadership at home is a light shining over your family. It means that when you shine over your family, you are leading your family from the dark to the light. It is how parents or guardians shine over their kids from birth until they graduate from college. Therefore, you shone over your kids from the day they were born to the day they graduated from college. The leadership you have shown by taking care of your kids is the light you shone over the kids. As soon as the child is born, you and your spouse assume leadership, role, and responsibility to take care of the child. Such duty never ends until the child graduates from college and secures employment. It's the leadership role and responsibility that you and your spouse invested in the child from birth. You shine over the child when you help the child crawl. You shone over the kids when you helped them to walk on their feet. You shone over the child when you sent the child to preschool, elementary, and high school, as well as college. When your children graduate from college, they will step into the community and shine across the town to continue with the leadership, role, and responsibility that affected them. While you shine over your home, you are shining over the entire community.

Leadership cannot be hidden.

You are the light of your community. "A city built on the hill cannot be hidden Matthew 5:14." You are the light: You cannot hide yourself in the community. Just as your light shines over the entire community, so your leadership signs over the entire community. While leadership is the light of society, it supplies you with a lens to visualize the internal and external environment of your community. You do not walk in the community assuming what is going on; you walk with clarity because you are the light. You shine over the area and see everything as you walk. You can see the big picture of your leadership environment and develop a system to assess issues as they come to your table. You must do the right thing. You must ensure that what you see in the community is what you are talking about in the city. Talk about your community and talk about yourself. It helps people in the community understand your leadership and gives you the support you need before you step into the leadership of the country.

Light, leadership, and community

Your leadership does not only shine for your home, but it also shines across the community. Your leadership is like the streetlights in the city. It shines over the city. Therefore, everybody in the city can use the light to their advantage. It gives people the opportunity to choose. The choice to work hard and succeed. It also helps people to use their talents for the good of society. People will walk out of self-pity and pursue their destined goals as farmers, engineers, accountants, or whatever trade or career they are destined to do. If you are destined to lead your country, you are well able to assume your leadership role and responsibility to lead your people in perspective. If you are destined to lead your country as a musician, Lawyer, cap driver, Medical Doctor, Hospital Nurse, or Custodian, do it to the best of your knowledge. It is how your leadership shone over people. Your leadership is not to encourage people to stay

home and get paid but to give people the opportunity to work and earn an income.

Gun control, leadership, role, and responsibility

What has blinded Congress over the past decade has also blinded the American public to think that gun control is to take guns from people to reduce mass killings, but it's not. Guns cannot walk or fly to people. Guns do not hate people. People hate people. If this is the case, why are you wasting time trying to figure out how to eliminate guns in society? Take your concerns away from guns and focus on people. You can take away all guns from people, but you cannot take away people from people. It's mental and psychological warfare. If you can overcome mental health deficiencies in people, you can overcome gun control.

Every gun incident in the United States involves people killing people using a gun. It does not involve guns killing people. Does the killer and the gun pose a threat to the people? Who is more dangerous to the public, the killer or the gun? The person committing violence is the most dangerous. Not the gun. In any deadliest incident, police always focus on the person who kills people. When the person is apprehended, then the police will begin to look for the gun. If the law enforcement officers focus on the person committing the crime, then let's all focus on the person committing the crime. Let's get to know more about these groups of people with mental health in society and their families. Let's consider the mentally challenged population as a disabled population and offer them support and some exceptions in most aspects of managing the challenges. The only way to reduce gun violence is to create mental health awareness across the country and educate families, business organizations, and organizations that deal with mental challenges, give them support, and have them share information with the authorities. It will help the authorities to help them better.

Mental health

One of the common illnesses that people hide from society is mental health sicknesses. Mental health has become the most hidden sickness in the public. People don't want to talk about it in the family, among friends, at workplaces, and even in public. Mental health sicknesses such as anger, stress, depression, anxiety, bipolar, etc., are sicknesses that are manageable like every other sickness in the world. Why can't you talk about mental health issues publicly in your home, with your friends, or at the workplace?

The reluctance to talk about mental health issues in public or in society and share information is a lack of awareness. People are not aware that when they communicate about their mental health issues to their loved ones, they are not only enhancing their lives but also, they are reducing gun violence. When you hide your mental sickness, including stress, anger, depression, anxiety, or bipolar, it will give birth to gun violence on the street. Because you don't get the treatment resources or support you need to be successful. If you and your family are hiding your mental illness, you are living in denial of being sick. You are putting yourself at risk of making the condition worse because you will lose the opportunity to receive public resources and support. Mental health is a public issue. It's not an individual issue. Therefore, everybody has a leadership role and responsibility to create mental health awareness in the area where they live, work, or do business. It will help ease pressure on people and allow them to voice out their mental health issues for support. Therefore, help create mental health awareness in your home, community, business, or workplace. It will make a difference in reducing gun violence.

Mental health is not a personal affair.

Mental health issues are not personal affairs. They are public affairs. Many people are giving up their mental health issues to violence, committing crimes, or losing jobs that can help them pay their bills. It is not a personal affair. It's public affairs. Mental health issues should not be kept secret. Keeping your mental health issues secret is frustrating. This is why a few people are giving up on their mental health to violence. Often, some mentally sick individuals take their frustrations up to their coworkers, bosses, college campuses, or their colleagues. It's also why high school or elementary students take their frustrations up to their teachers and fellow schoolchildren.

Not to forget, those more connected to public places take their frustrations to public places. Over the past few decades, many killings that occurred happened due to attachment. If this is what many people are going through individually, then the government must create public mental health awareness to support people suffering from the illness. The awareness must be clear and specific such that a mentally sick person knows and understands that illness is not a hidden issue. They are not in the illness alone. The awareness must assure them they can get help anywhere in their home, community, and workplaces. Giving this awareness to people with mental health illnesses will not only help them from giving up their lives to gun violence, but it will help them call for help when needed. When mentally sick persons know they can call their family, community hotline, or call their coworkers or supervisors for help, they will not look for a gun to kill and destroy others. However, they will feel supported, valued, and present. When mental health awareness is put in place to embody the sick, family, work, and the general society, the mentally sick person will not feel hopeless and be attracted to guns and violence. Therefore, creating mental health awareness will not only help ease tension in mentally sick people, but it will also create a pathway for them at home, workplaces, and in general society. It will help reduce gun violence.

Family mental health awareness.

Almost every gun violence in the United States involves people who have outstanding mental health issues. There's no doubt that these people have suffered alone with mental health issues before giving up to violence on the street. Most often, the gun person's family or parents know about the mental health issues way before the incident. But they have never wanted to talk about it in public. It is something secret that families do not talk about or tell the police. Families never want to notify the police about any concerns about their loved one's mental health issues. Because they feel like they are giving away their loved ones' privacy to the public, they consider mental health issues confidential to the public. Once you keep mental health issues private, you are depriving your loved one of getting the help they need from the government to manage mental health. You are putting your loved one in danger of suicide or killing themselves and others on the street. Your failure to share your loved one's mental health information led to them not getting enough help to function independently. This is why awareness is extremely critical to the mentally sick person, family, friends, and organizations that have workers with mental health disability. Mental health awareness will not only ease tension among people but also help people connect well in the community and workplaces.

How do you know about Confederate monuments and leadership roles and responsibilities?

Confederate monuments are not hated.

Are Confederacy and Confederate monuments a history or hate? When you define confederate monuments as hate, you have missed the opportunity to liberate the youth with history. How do you define history here in the United States? What is found alarming on the street today is the twit story about the Confederacy and the removal of Confederate monuments across the country. Over the years, Confederacy and Confederate monuments have been taught as part of history. However, the historical intentions behind the Confederacy and Confederate monuments have been overshadowed by political motives to flip what is history to hate.

Hate has become the theory about the Confederacy and Confederate monuments displayed on public property. If history is hated, why is history taught in the class? The only way you can learn about the past and present is through history. Any attempt to wipe out the Confederacy and Confederate monuments is an attempt to alter history. There is nothing like hate looking at a Confederate monument in the historic vicinity. How did you come to the conclusion that some historic monuments are hated? Confederated monuments are taken down across the country because people are politically convinced that the portrait reflects hate. Hate? I doubt. The only way history can resonate with hate is when it's not taught in class. People don't get to understand anything when they have not learned. It is critical to understand that history shapes policy. Chipping the walls of history can damage policies and put the next generation of leadership roles and responsibilities at risk. It undermines history, leadership, role, and responsibility.

Create a center for tourism in Confederate monuments.

Removing Confederate monuments from public places helped create a center for Confederate monuments to attract tourism. The youth deserve to know and understand that Confederacy and Confederate monuments are history. It helps the youth to embrace the legacy as history rather than hate and culture. It also helps the youth to develop a positive mindset towards the legacy. It's how history is celebrated. It's also the heart of leadership roles and responsibility. It takes leadership to educate the youth that Confederacy and Confederate monuments are not about anger, hate, and/or divisiveness but history to celebrate. It is not time to put statistics on the table of how people were mentally and psychologically wounded in the past.

It is also not time to add a new statistic by using the name of the Confederacy or Confederate monuments to commit a crime in society. Because nobody wants to promote such negative sparks of information in society, all these negative speeches about the past are poisoning the youth who have decided to promote legacy as history for the nation. It also poisons the minds of people who are already negative to continue to promote negativities about anger, hate, and divisiveness. Therefore, positive leadership, role, and responsibility are critical to assure people that the Confederacy is not about anger, hate, or divisiveness but history. It will help people avoid using confederate flags or signs to commit crimes in society. It will bring people together to celebrate history. In other words, it will wipe out hate and divisiveness not only in the community but also in politics. Living in the present of confederate monuments.

Confederate monuments are history does not hate. History helps us to know and understand the past, what happened in the past, why it happened, how it happened, and how it was resolved. History also helped us to learn from our mistakes. If the Confederacy needs to be wiped away from public places, then we are wiping away history. History is not hated. We learn the history of the past to gain knowledge and experience, but we don't live it. We do not learn and remain in it, or we do not gain any experience or knowledge. What to understand here is that when you learn history, you don't imitate people who created history and try to do the same in the present. If you do, you are learning and living in the past. You are not learning and living in the present. It means that you have not gained the knowledge, experience, and/or wisdom needed from what you learned in the past.

This is what many people who have used the Confederate flag to commit crimes in society did. They have learned the history of the Confederacy and Confederate monuments and have decided to live it. They want to fight the past war in the present. It is critical to let the youth know that we cannot live in the past. It is not our time to do so. Whatever happened in the past becomes history today. The monuments, names of streets, or properties that were named by the Confederate leaders are history. This is our time. It is our time to be positive, preserve everything that talks about the Confederacy, and educate people about the horrific things that happened during the Confederacy and how leaders show leadership, role, and responsibility in transforming it to this better future. With this, we can preserve a healthy history of the Confederacy without anger, hate, and divisiveness. It will help people talk to their children about the Confederate leaders or Confederacy as history does not hate. It will also help politicians to preserve Confederate monuments at decent locations for tourism. It is the heart of leadership, role, and responsibility.

Confederate monuments as education.

Whatever history is, education is not personal. Confederate monuments are history to educate the youth and the next generation of people. Since the removal of Confederate monuments, many people have taken it personally. Both supporters and non-supporters took it personally. It is usual to feel that way in every predictable situation. But if you dwell in it, you do not get to preserve the heritage in a way that will help society. Because your anger is going to scare people who would have loved to promote it, take leadership, role, and responsibility to preserve the monuments by creating the center for Confederate monuments where all Confederate monuments are decorated for tourism. Let it be education but not anger, hate, and divisiveness. Do not label the monuments as hate but as history. Do not label yourself with anger, hate, and divisiveness about Confederate monuments because they are history. History does not belong to one person. It belongs to everybody. Therefore, do not label yourself to fight a new confederacy in the present. Do not remove them, either. Label yourself with leadership, role, and responsibility. Label yourself as a role model to love, not to hate, to unite, not to divide. In this way, people will collectively support history and help decorate the center for Confederate monuments. Therefore, do not remove monuments, do not fight a new confederacy, do not alter someone else's history to make your history, and do not carry someone else's cross, but carry your own cross (Luke 9:23). It helps people live united. It's the vision of the United States of America.

Covering history from youth.

History is not to pursue the past but to enhance the present. The removal of the Confederate monuments is the act of covering history from the youth. While history is protected to help the youth uncover the values of the past, politicians are wiping off history by removing Confederate monuments and renaming properties. Regardless of the motives, confederate monuments have become history. This history is valuable for the youth to learn and know about the past of the country. History will also help the youth to understand how civilization ministered from slavery to emancipation and to the present. Even as the Confederacy is over, the key characters of the Confederacy must remain fresh in the minds of all Americans because of the history that was created. The characters make up the story of the Confederacy. Due to this, confederate monuments are critical in the history of the Confederacy and the nation. Therefore, displaying the monuments of these characters will motivate the youth to assess the spectrum of leadership roles and responsibilities of the past and navigate through it with the new culture of the United States of America.

It is the heart of leadership, role, and responsibility. Maximize your leadership. Do not maximize hate by covering history from youth. There will always be one person in society who will use every good thing to justify hate. This is what happened to the Confederacy and Confederate monuments. Due to a few people using Confederate flags to justify killings, society perceived the Confederacy as hated. It's all politics. Do not let your mind dwell on the actions of a few small-minded individuals who use the confederate flag to commit a crime. Those people had planned to kill. However, they were not born to hate. They were born to lead. They are destined to lead the people that they killed. Unfortunately, they kill them. It is too late to save the lives of those killed, but it's not too late to stop using the Confederate flags to justify war in the present. Let us find a place where we can house these historical figures, decorate the area, and allow for tourism.

Confederacy and slavery.

While we try to preserve history, walk away from hate, divisiveness, humiliation, and fresh memory of the Confederacy and slavery. Confederacy and slavery are history. Do not make them current in your home, workplace, or in your business. Do not allow the anger, divisiveness, and hate about confederation and slavery to overshadow your ambition to pursue the values of the nation, leadership, role, and responsibility. Do not assume your leadership role and responsibility with anger, hate, and divisive mindset of the past. Confederacy and slavery have become a lasting history that needs to be passed on from generation to generation. Do not destroy history. Learn, understand, and preserve history. History is education. As you learn from your parents and grandparents, so your kids and grandkids are going to learn from you, too. The only way you can educate the youth is to tell them the truth, and the truth will set them free (John 8:32). This is what the scripture says. You cannot cover history from youth and expect them to learn about the past. Where are they going to learn history? It's like dropping your wallet in Las Vegas and looking for it in Washington. How can you find it? How will the youth understand the history of the Confederacy and slavery if you cover them? History is what happened yesterday. Whatever happened yesterday is gone, but what we learn about it is what we are talking about today. It's the heart of history. I have experienced slavery history covered in my family. My granddad and his first cousin were captured in slavery, but my family covered the history. Due to this, only a handful of people in my family know about this story, and a majority of them have not been told the full story.

History of slavery in my family.

After the abolitionists of slavery had already decided to end slavery in Europe, my granddad and his first cousin were captured and taken into slavery. My granddad came back home after many years in slavery, but his first cousin never came back home. It was a traumatic situation and story in my family during this time. It became a story that my family didn't want to talk about in the open, even though it was not a secret. Nobody in my family at that time had been to school. Therefore, they did not understand the significance of history. They covered the story and did not want anybody in the family to talk about it. They covered the story at home, but they could not cover it in the community. As time passed, my family thought they were covering it, but the information had already spread in an incredibly distinct way from one generation to the other. Yes, they destroyed the evidence, but the story is still in the air. At that time, any story about slavery in my family was not fun, but it was history. While slavery was not a fun story in my family, nobody in the family had committed a crime using anger or hate as a justification for our grandparents being taken into slavery. According to my Dad, the family became more united after my grandpa and his cousin were captured. They called for peace in the family. They reached out to each other when needed. It was how they got out of the humiliation, frustration, and feeling of loss. I have no doubt that this nightmare was the leading reason why they tried to hide the story.

Shredded evidence after my granddad passed away.

After my granddad had passed away, my Dad and his brothers decided to dispose of my granddad's stuff that they did not need. At that time, I had just come back from school, and my Dad and his brothers were sitting on the front porch with my granddad's small wooden box to dispose of it. As usual, my Dad joked with me and said open the box and tell me what you find. I quickly opened the box and pulled out something like a shirt, and there were patches on the back that said "slave worker." I read it aloud and asked them what that was, and one of my uncles quickly ordered that I should put everything back in the box, and I did. They disposed of it. None of them told me anything until I was on the farm with my Dad, and he told me everything about it.

Having received this news, I was devastated. My granddad had already passed away. I would not be able to ask him questions that matter to me about slavery. My Dad did not want me to ask any of his brothers about this story because they agreed to cover the story. However, I went to one of my uncle's only surviving grandkids at that time, who was older than my Dad, and asked him if he could tell me what happened to my granddad and my granduncle. He explained the story even better than I heard from my Dad. He walked me into his room and showed me an animal skin jacket hanging on the wall that belonged to my granduncle.

And he asked me to touch it, and I did. Then he told me,

"Your granduncle is still here; we don't talk about it."

Mental health at workplaces

Mental health awareness at the workplace is critical to keep mentally sick individuals connected at work. If the government encourages organizations to implement mental health awareness and disclosure policies in place for organizations to manage mentally sick staff, it will change the entire atmosphere of gun control. It will also change the atmosphere of the employee. Employers are always hiring and keeping people to work and advance the business, but if they don't know about employee's health needs, they don't get to help them better. How much can your employers help you if they don't know more about your mental health issues? To help employers help their mentally sick staff manage work and mental health, the government needs to encourage mental health awareness policy at workplaces.

The policy will define the level of help employers need to help their employees. Allow employers to receive medical reports and have the right to follow up with their employees if they are taking their medications. It will not only allow mentally sick employees to open up to their employers, but it will also help employers to welcome them to the business and have them make it a career. It will enhance employer-employee relationships. It will help mentally disabled employees to get motivated to take their health management seriously, take their medications as prescribed, and follow up with their physicians regularly. This will help them work every week, earn an income, and be able to pay their bills and support their families. Apart from this, they will not lose their jobs, lack the care they need, fall into homelessness or hopelessness, and take the frustration to the street.

How do you know about Confederate monuments and leadership roles and responsibilities?

Confederate monuments are not hated.

Are Confederacy and Confederate monuments a history or hate? When you define confederate monuments as hate, you have missed the opportunity to liberate the youth with history. How do you define history here in the United States? What is found alarming on the street today is the twit story about the Confederacy and the removal of Confederate monuments across the country. Over the years, Confederacy and Confederate monuments have been taught as part of history. However, the historical intentions behind the Confederacy and Confederate monuments have been overshadowed by political motives to flip what is history to hate.

Hate has become the theory about the Confederacy and Confederate monuments displayed on public property. If history is hated, why is history taught in the class? The only way you can learn about the past and present is through history. Any attempt to wipe out the Confederacy and Confederate monuments is an attempt to alter history. There is nothing like hate looking at a Confederate monument in the historic vicinity. How did you come to the conclusion that some historic monuments are hated? Confederated monuments are taken down across the country because people are politically convinced that the portrait reflects hate. Hate? I doubt. The only way history can resonate with hate is when it's not taught in class. People don't get to understand anything when they have not learned. It is critical to understand that history shapes policy. Chipping the walls of history can damage policies and put the next generation of leadership roles and responsibilities at risk. It undermines history, leadership, role, and responsibility.

Create a center for tourism in Confederate monuments.

Removing Confederate monuments from public places helped create a center for Confederate monuments to attract tourism. The youth deserve to know and understand that Confederacy and Confederate monuments are history. It helps the youth to embrace the legacy as history rather than hate and culture. It also helps the youth to develop a positive mindset towards the legacy. It's how history is celebrated. It's also the heart of leadership roles and responsibility. It takes leadership to educate the youth that Confederacy and Confederate monuments are not about anger, hate, and/or divisiveness but history to celebrate. It is not time to put statistics on the table of how people were mentally and psychologically wounded in the past.

It is also not time to add a new statistic by using the name of the Confederacy or Confederate monuments to commit a crime in society. Because nobody wants to promote such negative sparks of information in society, all these negative speeches about the past are poisoning the youth who have decided to promote legacy as history for the nation. It also poisons the minds of people who are already negative to continue to promote negativities about anger, hate, and divisiveness. Therefore, positive leadership, role, and responsibility are critical to assure people that the Confederacy is not about anger, hate, or divisiveness but history. It will help people avoid using confederate flags or signs to commit crimes in society. It will bring people together to celebrate history. In other words, it will wipe out hate and divisiveness not only in the community but also in politics. Living in the present of confederate monuments.

Confederate monuments are history does not hate. History helps us to know and understand the past, what happened in the past, why it happened, how it happened, and how it was resolved. History also helped us to learn from our mistakes. If the Confederacy needs to be wiped away from public places, then we are wiping away history. History is not hated. We learn the history of the past to gain knowledge and experience, but we don't live it. We do not learn and remain in it, or we do not gain any experience or knowledge. What to understand here is that when you learn history, you don't imitate people who created history and try to do the same in the present. If you do, you are learning and living in the past. You are not learning and living in the present. It means that you have not gained the knowledge, experience, and/or wisdom needed from what you learned in the past.

This is what many people who have used the Confederate flag to commit crimes in society did. They have learned the history of the Confederacy and Confederate monuments and have decided to live it. They want to fight the past war in the present. It is critical to let the youth know that we cannot live in the past. It is not our time to do so. Whatever happened in the past becomes history today. The monuments, names of streets, or properties that were named by the Confederate leaders are history. This is our time. It is our time to be positive, preserve everything that talks about the Confederacy, and educate people about the horrific things that happened during the Confederacy and how leaders show leadership, role, and responsibility in transforming it to this better future. With this, we can preserve a healthy history of the Confederacy without anger, hate, and divisiveness. It will help people talk to their children about the Confederate leaders or Confederacy as history does not hate. It will also help politicians to preserve Confederate monuments at decent locations for tourism. It is the heart of leadership, role, and responsibility.

Confederate monuments as education.

Whatever history is, education is not personal. Confederate monuments are history to educate the youth and the next generation of people. Since the removal of Confederate monuments, many people have taken it personally. Both supporters and non-supporters took it personally. It is usual to feel that way in every predictable situation. But if you dwell in it, you do not get to preserve the heritage in a way that will help society. Because your anger is going to scare people who would have loved to promote it, take leadership, role, and responsibility to preserve the monuments by creating the center for Confederate monuments where all Confederate monuments are decorated for tourism. Let it be education but not anger, hate, and divisiveness. Do not label the monuments as hate but as history. Do not label yourself with anger, hate, and divisiveness about Confederate monuments because they are history. History does not belong to one person. It belongs to everybody. Therefore, do not label yourself to fight a new confederacy in the present. Do not remove them, either. Label yourself with leadership, role, and responsibility. Label yourself as a role model to love, not to hate, to unite, not to divide. In this way, people will collectively support history and help decorate the center for Confederate monuments. Therefore, do not remove monuments, do not fight a new confederacy, do not alter someone else's history to make your history, and do not carry someone else's cross, but carry your own cross (Luke 9:23). It helps people live united. It's the vision of the United States of America.

Covering history from youth.

History is not to pursue the past but to enhance the present. The removal of the Confederate monuments is the act of covering history from the youth. While history is protected to help the youth uncover the values of the past, politicians are wiping off history by removing Confederate monuments and renaming properties. Regardless of the motives, confederate monuments have become history. This history is valuable for the youth to learn and know about the past of the country. History will also help the youth to understand how civilization ministered from slavery to emancipation and to the present. Even as the Confederacy is over, the key characters of the Confederacy must remain fresh in the minds of all Americans because of the history that was created. The characters make up the story of the Confederacy. Due to this, confederate monuments are critical in the history of the Confederacy and the nation. Therefore, displaying the monuments of these characters will motivate the youth to assess the spectrum of leadership roles and responsibilities of the past and navigate through it with the new culture of the United States of America.

It is the heart of leadership, role, and responsibility. Maximize your leadership. Do not maximize hate by covering history from youth. There will always be one person in society who will use every good thing to justify hate. This is what happened to the Confederacy and Confederate monuments. Due to a few people using Confederate flags to justify killings, society perceived the Confederacy as hated. It's all politics. Do not let your mind dwell on the actions of a few small-minded individuals who use the confederate flag to commit a crime. Those people had planned to kill. However, they were not born to hate. They were born to lead. They are destined to lead the people that they killed. Unfortunately, they kill them. It is too late to save the lives of those killed, but it's not too late to stop using the Confederate flags to justify war in the present. Let us find a place where we can house these historical figures, decorate the area, and allow for tourism.

My granddad and his first cousins lived before they were captured for slavery.

My granduncle and my granddad both lived in different areas of the countryside. These areas were all farmlands, and they built their homes on the farm. Both were young, married and lived with their spouses. However, my granduncle and Granddad were both captured in the same month, ten days apart, but by two separate groups of people. My granddad was captured in the first week of the month, and my granduncle in the 2nd week of the month. My granddad came home after slavery, but his first cousin never came back home. According to the story, they never met anywhere in any of the slavery camps.

My grand uncle's family life

According to the story, my uncle was the first child of his parents. He did not go to school, but he was educated how to manage a farm. My granduncle had a large farm, built his home on the farm, and lived with his wife and four little kids. According to the story, it was harvesting season, and he was on the farm harvesting grains. It was midday, and my grand uncle's wife had prepared lunch for him. After my granduncle had finished eating the meal and was about to go back to the field, a group of people circled around the field with horses and guns and took my granduncle into slavery, leaving his wife on the farm. His wife cried home and told the family that her husband was captured and taken away.

The family rushed to the area, but they had taken him away. According to the story, my granduncle was a farmer and a hardworking man who cared for his family. He was a successful farmer has a lot of cattle and fowl on the farm. Like everybody else, my granduncle was enjoying his youth with his family, wife, and four children. He has no business with anybody, but he was captured on the farm. He did not get to see his wife and four children again. From the day he was captured to this date, my family never heard of him. My granduncle never came back home, but my granddad was fortunately dismissed from slavery, and he returned home.

My granddad's life

According to my Dad, my granddad and his sister were kids when their father passed away, leaving them with their mother. Their mother remarried in the family and had help to raise my granddad and his sister. Like everybody else, my granddad grew up in a lovely family. He was a hardworking young man and had just married a beautiful girl and had his first child. He moved with his wife to a new home on the farm.

According to my Dad, my granddad had a lot of cattle and a small flock on the farm. Also, he was given the entire farm that his Dad had left behind. As young as my granddad was, he managed the farms very well and always had a good harvest. According to my Dad, my granddad was enjoying life as everybody does at the time, working on his farm and taking care of his wife and infant child. However, he was captured while he was harvesting grains on the farm. On this day, a group of people circled his farm with their horses and guns and captured him to slavery. According to the story, this group of people attempted to go with him and his wife and only child, but his wife was sick with what is now known as chickenpox. When they discovered that this girl was sick, they left her in the forest with the baby, and she walked home and spread the news. From this day, this girl suffered a panic attack and humiliation and shortly passed away, leaving her son, who was later raised by my grandad's half-brother. After many years in slavery, my granddad was dismissed from slavery, and he returned home.

The return of my granddad

The Unfolding story about my granddad's experience in slavery was fascinating, but I cannot elaborate on it here. The first thing my granddad told the family on arrival was that "Slavery is purposeful, lack of leadership, but my capture is a history." This piece of information gained roots in the family at that time. According to my Dad, the family lived to understand that slavery was a purposeful lack of leadership, but my granddad's capture was history. According to my Granddad, he never thought he would be released from slavery to come home because he was forced to work hard for a daily meal, water to drink, and water to shower. My granddad stated that after he was captured and transported abroad, he was recruited into a team to build railroads.

Over the years, according to my granddad, he successfully learned the trade to construct railroads. He works and can help other team members get the work done on time. His supervisors were good to him. He helped with many railroad constructions and was good at the job. Due to this, they took him across the sea again to help with more railroad construction. At this time, he realized he was in Africa. In Africa, he helped with railroad construction in many separate places.

During this time, he was too old to do anything, but he was directing the younger ones the right way to get work done. Fortunately, he said his captives were recruiting new people every day to work until the last railway line was completed. At this time, he was appointed with other people as a night security guard to guard the staff and properties at night. According to my Granddad, while in this job, many of his supervisors retired, and when they were about to leave, they dismissed him with other friends to go home.

My granddad journeyed back home.

After the dismissal, my granddad said he did not know where to go. In town, he met a few people who came from areas that he had heard about before. So, he teamed up with them, and they took off with the horses and guns that were given to them. They went through the forest, crossed rivers with their horses, passed through villages, and asked people for directions to areas that they had heard about before. The journey, he said, was rough and wild. They eat and sleep in the forest. They used the horses to hunt for food in the forest. A few days into the journey, one of them got sick and could not ride his horse. This person was the only one on the team who spoke the same language as my granddad. According to the story, my granddad left the sick man's horse behind in the forest, and my granddad carried the sick person with him. They finally entered a familiar forest and appeared in a village where one of them understood the language. They had the sick person treated for a few days, and they continued the journey. At this time, they got to understand exactly the geographical location of the area and where they needed to go from then. Unfortunately, they came from different areas and must be separated at that point. He left with the sick person who was recovering well from the sickness and went to the area where this person came from. With directions, they found the sick person's home. From there, he left with his horse and continued the journey, finally finding his way home.

My granddad's arrival at home

My granddad came home and found out that his wife had passed away many years ago through panic attacks, humiliation, stress, and the feeling of the loss of her husband. My granddad grieved for the loss of his wife. However, his son, who was less than a year old at the time he was captured, had married and had children and grandchildren. My granddad reunited with his son, grandchildren, and great-grandchildren. While he was happy to meet his family, he was not excited because his son appeared too old than himself because he was always sick. Eventually, the son passed away, leaving him with the kids.

However, upon my granddad's return from slavery, he married two girls, including my Dad's mother. My Dad's mother had three children, and the other girl had two children. After this, my granddad was too old for his wives to produce children. However, the two women teamed up together and took care of my granddad and the children. Growing up, my Dad had an enjoyable time with my granddad. He was always there when my granddad needed him. According to my Dad, every season had a set of stories that my granddad told him.

My granddad will tell him stories about his experience in slavery and recommend that he not tell people. However, my Dad said my granddad would generally call his wives and children and offer them advice. According to my Dad, my granddad often tells them to learn how to love, not hate. He told them, "Hate is weakness, lack of knowledge, lack of understanding, lack of wisdom, and lack of love." He also told them to forgive in every situation, even if it does not make sense, because he said, "It shows leadership." My granddad came back after slavery full of wisdom because he was self-educated in the process. Due to this, he transformed the entire family into a new culture of relationships, unity, leadership, and responsibility. According to my Dad, my granddad always prays for his friends who did not make it home after slavery. My Dad said before my granddad passed away, he prayed for his friends who died in slavery and never got to see their families again. He prayed for many people who died right in front of his face because of panic and heart attack, while others died in the course of the work and fatigue associated with weather and illnesses.

None of my parents could read and write.

My Dad and his four wives never went to school. They could not read or write. My Dad told me that he was only taught how to manage a farm. With this basic education, my Dad was able to successfully manage his poor farm. The farm was not fertile and could only do well with fertilizer and adequate rain. My Dad will always buy fertilizer, but the rain is not consistent and will not fall at the right time. Due to these rain issues, my parents will work hard to keep the farm, yet they will often have poor harvests. Because the land was not fertile, and no crop wanted to grow on it. My Dad would tell me that this rain issue was not new to him. He would also say that he was aware of the rain problems, but only God could allow rain anytime He wanted. Regardless of my Dad's experience in farming, he often gets poor harvests due to the inconsistency of the rainfall. However, my Dad often has enough harvest for the family. The funniest thing about my Dad's farming was that none of the crops they grew on the farm were used for commercial purposes. Everything that my parents harvested from the farm goes for family consumption. They never had savings or checking accounts, but they were always united.

The family was together.

There was nothing big to boast about in my family more than the love, care, and unity that overshadowed the entire family's vision to stay together. I would think that there would be no peace in my Dad home since he married four women and lived with all of them in the same house. But my Dad's house was the most peaceful home in which to live. I was loved in the house, cared for, and supported by my Dad and mother. I cannot recollect any bad encounter I ever had with them. I still remember most of the good encounters that I had experienced with them: The love, care, and support I received from them. My parents made the relationships in our family impossible, such as not smiling, saying hi to each other when we woke up from bed, or asking people if they needed help. It is the kind of life my parents lived. They implemented the love, care, and unity that I enjoyed in the family. Every one of my parents made up their mind to be positive in the relationship, at home, with the children, and with the people in the community. Today, I believe my parents' positive behavior in their relationship is the reason why me and my siblings are together. It was the culture of the family to love, care, and support each other regardless of any adversity. This behavior promoted the family's vision to live together.

Togetherness.

While the family was known for its love, care, and support for each other, the family's culture of togetherness was outstanding. It was shocking how my parents promoted togetherness in the family while in such a relationship of one man with four wives. Regardless of my parents' married situation, they always plan and do things together. Growing up, I began to appreciate my parents' efforts in collaborating ideas, promoting togetherness, and standing for the interests of the family and not their individual interests. My parents' leadership inspired me. When I reflect on their family leadership, it appears to me like it is one of the kinds. Many people today cannot live with one woman or man forever. Today, only a few married relationships last forever, but the majority end up in separation and/or divorce. Reflecting on this gives me the opportunity to talk more about my parents' relationship and how they promoted togetherness in the family. It was remarkable how every one of my parents understood the relationship and upheld collaboration as the hallmark of their relationship. They often invite me and my siblings to any project that they are working on, either on the farm or at home. Such family behavior helped me partner with my Dad at home, in the community, and on the farm, and I learned from him.

I followed my Dad everywhere he went.

Growing up, I loved to follow my Dad wherever he went and listen to his stories. Whether at home, in the community, or on the farm, I followed my Dad and learned from him. My Dad will tell me many stories. Stories about himself, his family, and the community. My Dad will tell me how he loves the family and community. He tells me that everybody in his family and the community deserves love. He will tell me how special I am to him, how my siblings are special, my mothers, and the people in the community. He tells me that we all make his day every day. My Dad will tell me that it is good to be happy with your family and community. He tells me that good family behavior promotes a healthy community and vice versa. My Dad does not get tired of telling positive stories.

Sometimes, on the farm, he will let us walk around the farm for a few minutes and take a break. We will go and sit under a big shea nut tree that we had on the farm. He will tell me all the good stories that he wants to tell me because I love stories. Sometimes, I would ask my Dad for stories. My Dad does not forget what he told me today or what he told me a few days or months ago. He will repeat them repeatedly just to make sure I remember to say them or repeat them with him. My Dad stories were not just stories but theories. They were reflective. I came to know most of my Dad's theories and could tell them without hesitation. I did enjoy the best of my Dad, and I miss him.

My Dad's theories.

I learned and understood my Dad the same way many people did. I listened to his stories and theories, and I used them as a guide to navigate through my own life. My Dad had five principles that he talked to me about each time I was with him at home or on the farm. My Dad will always tell me to learn and not be the same, work with everybody in mind, help others if I can, be willing to work and earn an income and be a leader of my community. As a child, this simple education from my Dad was enough to affect my life, the way I live with my parents and siblings at home, how I partner with my friends and navigate life in the community, and how I respect myself and teachers at school. Such a behavior enhanced my social life and shaped my mindset to respect people the way I see them. Today, it helps me to respect my neighbors in the community, my bosses at work, my coworkers, my friends, and the people I supervise and interact with to get my work done. The positive advice and encouragement I received from my Dad empowered me to take my daily leadership, role, and responsibility as the hallmark of my integrity.

Learn and do not be the same.

My Dad often tells me to "Learn and do not be the same." My Dad did not go to school. So, when he tells me to learn and not be the same, he tells me not to do the same things that he did and fail. My Dad often works hard on the farm and loves to recommend the best farming practices that he thinks will work well if I pursue it. He will divide the land into several acres according to the type of crops that he wants to grow on them. The most common crops that he grows on the farm are millet, corn, rice, and beans. My Dad will walk me through all the areas of the land and show me why millet, corn, and beans can grow in the same area and rice cannot. He tells me to walk around the farm and see how the crops grow. It will help me get some clues about how to shift them in the next season. He will explain to me how he does his work and the effort he puts into keeping the farm.

Also, he tells me how the rain fails him every year and causes him to have poor harvests in every season. Most importantly, he tells me how he spent the entire of his life on the same farm, and yet he gains nothing but the food he brings home to feed the family. Then, my Dad would ask me, "Do you want to spend your entire life doing the same thing that I did on this farm?" I would say no, and then my Dad would tell me, "Learn and do not be the same." My Dad did not stop here, and he told me to work with everybody in mind.

Work with everybody in mind.

My Dad developed this theory during this time that many farmers were using chemicals to produce most of the vegetables. There were those kinds of rumors going on that people were sick because farmers were spraying a lot of chemicals on vegetables to prevent insects from eating them. However, they harvest these vegetables and sell them to consumers, causing many consumers to get sick. My Dad was worrying about how the chemicals in vegetables could affect consumers' health. However, he spoke about three things: Farming and market, family and community, and community. My Dad believes that these three things are tied up together, and he needs to have them in mind while he works on his farm. He would tell me that the farm, market, family, and community are all about people, and when you are dealing with anything that is connected to society, you must do it with consciousness. Because he says, it accounts for your integrity. I believe it also accounts for your leadership, role, and responsibility because it's the heart of leadership.

Farming and the market.

My Dad spoke about the need for collaboration in the farming and the market community to ensure that the amount of chemicals used in vegetable production is adequate. Often, he would tell me that it is right for all farmers to embrace collaboration, learn from each other, and engage in good farming practices. He would tell me that it was critical for all farmers to collaborate on ideas, skills, and knowledge about using chemicals for farming so that they can produce not only plenty of food but also food that is right for consumers. This is because he says farmers supply food to consumers. He said farmers should not run out of supply or lack quality food to supply the market.

Due to many unskilled farmers using chemicals to grow vegetables at that time, these emphases were needed in the area to help farmers adopt approaches that were right for each season to produce plenty of quality food. Even though my Dad did not collect data to determine the number of people who were positively affected by his efforts in the area, I believe it was a good act of encouraging farming communities to collaborate and produce quality products for the market or consumers. My Dad believed that farmers reach everybody on the table and must be encouraged to control the use of chemicals in vegetable production. He would tell me to work with everybody in mind.

Family and community.

My Dad often emphasizes the need to work with family and the community in mind. He says they are "your life partners." While you work for your family, he says, also think of your community because whatever hits your family can also affect the community and vice versa. I used to watch how my Dad and his four wives collaborate with ideas and develop plans for the family and the farm. They will call to the table, discuss issues, and plan. They will not take minutes because none of them went to school or could read and write. My Dad cares for the opinions of his wives, and they work together to ensure that they execute their plans as planned. My parents always have different farming plans for each year based on the weather information.

My Dad positively interacted with the community and his four wives all the time. During the farming season, he would collaborate with his wives as well as other farmers in the community. He used to have an authoritative voice, but it was normal to his wives, me, and the community. Everybody likes him in town. I was going along with him almost 99.9 percent of the time. He will tell me how critical it was to care for his family and community. He said caring for his family and community does not mean he has to provide everything they need to show it, but it means he must be open to them, collaborate with them, be honest, and be fair to them in every action. He says your family and community are your partners, friends, and key mentors in your lifetime, and you must be proud of them. He says your family and community are your backbone.

Community.

According to my Dad, it is critical to collaborate with the community in mind. He said your home is your tail, and the community is your head. He would say things like whatever activity or actions that you do/take at home can manifest in the community. In other words, whatever you produce on your farm will be sold in the community. Therefore, it was critical to collaborate with the community in mind. Living in a small farming community, my Dad knows everybody in town. He also knows everything that is going on in the community. My Dad will try to visit everybody in the community by the end of each week. Whether it was rainy season or dry season, my Dad would spare time to check on everybody in the community. Often, I don't see the community members visiting my Dad as he does.

Most often, the community members visit my Dad only when there is a problem in the town. Sometimes, I would ask my Dad why he visits every family in the community daily, weekly, or monthly. My Dad will tell me that when he doesn't spend time with his community members, he is not connected with the community. He says it was extremely critical for him to connect with the community members so that he could get to know them better. He also says it helps him to understand them and develop a plan for the community. He says you cannot develop the community without having much knowledge about the community. With more knowledge, he says, you can plan how you want the community to look socially, economically, and politically. Now, he says he visits families in the community also because he wants to know how everybody is doing and ensure that they know what is going on in the community. He said the community belongs to everybody living in the community, but not everybody in the community cares about the community. This does not mean he says you should not care about your community. He would tell me to take leadership, role, and responsibility for the community, develop it if I can, and allow everybody to join the process. Then he would tell me, "Help others if you can."

Help others if you can.

One of my Dad's favorite theories was "Help others if you can." Here, it was difficult for me to understand my Dad's position about what he meant about this theory. Even when my Dad needed me to help my siblings with their school homework assignments, he would tell me to help others if I could. Even though my Dad believes that helping others is an independent decision, he also believes that it takes leadership to help others. He says helping others does not mean you should feed them every day but helping people with skills and opportunities to earn income. My Dad used to live in a remote area of the town where schools were not accessible to people in the area.

Most people living in those areas at that time did not go to school. They were all traditional agricultural or local farmers. They learned from their parents or grandparents to manage the farms. They did not get any formal education or training in farming. Based on this, most of them did not adequately time the farming seasons. However, they had only one season of the year to do agricultural farming. Therefore, food shortages in the area were common. If your crops do not do well in the season, you are most likely to experience food shortage. Many people used to experience food shortages at that time. They will come to my Dad and ask for food supplies to their homes. My Dad and his wives would consult with each other and supply them with any little food they could get. Then, my Dad will educate them about the behavior of the rainy season and tell them to collaborate with the farming experts and pay attention to updates about the season, when to start, and when to finish. As always, my Dad will tell everybody to be willing to work and earn an income.

Be willing to work and earn an income.

It was my Dad's routine message to people: "Be willing to work and earn an income." At home or on the farm, my Dad will tell me the need to work and earn an income. This was my Dad's message to friends, people in the community, and everybody that comes across him. Regardless of the lack of jobs in the area and poor rainy behavior to do farming work, my Dad would still encourage people to work. My Dad believes that everybody deserves to work and earn an income at some point. He believes that everybody has a leadership role and responsibility to work for themselves or for others and earn an income.

He will tell me story upon story why everybody needs to work. His primary theory was that nothing free falls from the sky. Food does not fall from the sky. He will tell me that God blessed people with some skills to work in many ways.so God allows rain to fall from the sky and wet the land so that those who are farmers can engage on the farm. But God will not do the farming for you. he says you must develop the land and cultivate crops by yourself. But he will tell me that "God does not farm, but he grows the crops for you on the farm." And he would tell me to be willing to work and earn an income. As you work and earn income, you can take care of yourself, your family, and the community. While telling people to be willing to work and earn an income, he also tells people to become leaders of the community.

Be a leader of your community.

Here, my Day's view of being a leader of the community was based on four areas of leadership: It was based on (1) my Dad's principles, (2) your effort to help develop a healthy community, (3) Helping children to develop a positive bond with family and the community, and (4) Develop positive relationships with the community. If you live close to my Dad, you do not have any questions about how to remember my Dad's theories and stories. Because his theories and stories were his daily conversations, he would talk about them right when the situation popped up or when he walked into the situation with you. It could be at home, on the farm, in a shopping center, or at any social gathering. He will always find something wrong to talk about it. He will talk about his simple leadership principles.

Leadership based on principles.

My Dad definition of a leader in the community was based on his principles: learn and do not be the same, work with other people in mind, help others if you can, be willing to work and earn an income and be a leader of your community. From my Dad's perspective, leaders must be willing to learn and enhance their leadership skills and practices every day. Leaders must collaborate with their staff and be willing to work and support the community. My Dad often tells me that supporting the community does not mean you must share everything that you have with everybody in the community. But you must embrace the community as your partner, connect with the people, understand the needs of the people and the community, set up the community-building goal, and develop a plan for how you can collaborate with the people to achieve them.

My Dad says leading your community's family is mental work. He says you must mentally set your mind to take the leadership, role, and responsibility of the community. It is how you can support the community. It is also how you can bring the people in the community together and help them build the community. Therefore, he says this is the best way you can help develop a healthy community.

Help build a healthy community.

Even though my Dad did not go to school and could not read and write, his message to people was to "help build a healthy community." A healthy community, in my Dad's perspective, is a community where people are connected and communicate about the community, empowering the youth while taking their leadership role and responsibility judiciously. According to my Dad, when you have a common bond with the youth, family, and leadership in the community, you are going to have a positive relationship in the city. My Dad understands that a healthy community needs healthy leadership that can bring people in the community together. My Dad believes that when he helps people understand the need to learn and collaborate with others in the community, they will help develop a positive bond with the community and their family. Based on this, he says that when every family develops a positive mindset in the community, they will not only set up a solid foundation for the children but also promote a healthy community for the youth.

Help children develop a positive bond with the family and community.

My Dad had a passion for helping children develop a positive bond with the family and community. With this, my Dad will advise his friends and everybody who comes across his way repeatedly. He tells people to allow their children to enroll in community programs and help them engage in activities that are healthy, inspire them to love their family and the community and help them discover their potential in leadership. My Dad would tell me not to spend time yelling at children at home. Instead, enroll them in the community programs. My Dad believes that when you link your kids to community programs, they will interact with peers, learn new skills, and develop a positive bond not only with the community but also with the family. He always allows me and my siblings to join our peers in the community.

One time I went with my Dad to drop off roofing materials to a client in another city. When we arrived, my Dad and I saw the client yelling and shouting at his kids. I thought he was fighting an enemy, but when we walked close to him, I saw kids kneeling at the corner while he yelled and shouted at them. My Dad quickly asked me to step back so that he could advise the client. When I was about to step back, I heard my Dad telling the client to stop yelling and shouting at the children. He asked his client to let the children get up and go, and the client did. My Dad told his client to assign the children to any community program. He told him to engage the kids with activities in town. He believes that it will keep the kids occupied and will also model them to voluntarily take responsibility for the family. In other words, they would be motivated to learn new things, be nice to their parents, and be willing to help them at home. He also told the client that children learn while they grow. Therefore, he says you need to connect your children to activities in the community.

Develop positive relationships with your family and the community.

My Dad often encourages people to develop positive relationships with the family and community. He believes that a positive relationship with the family and community is critical for a healthy community. At home, my Dad would tell me to love my community as much as I love my home. If you love your family and you don't love your community, you are committed to vulnerability. Your world starts from your home, but it ends up in the community. Therefore, develop love in your community. My Dad will go further and tell me that loving your community does not mean you should worship the people in the community, but care for them. It shows leadership. What My Dad really means here is that building the community begins with you. Like everybody else, you are inclusive in community development. It means that you have the leadership role and responsibility to develop your relationship with the community by connecting with the people. You must collaborate with people, plan with them, and bring them together to build the community. It is the heart of leadership, role, and responsibility.

Misconceptions.

When I was growing up, I thought every family in my Dad's community believed in my Dad's principles: learn and do not be the same, work with other people in mind, help others if you can, be willing to work and earn an income, and be a leader of your community, but it was completely the opposite. People didn't want to talk about these principles to their families and help the kids learn and know about their community. Many children in the community did not know anything about these principles. I met with many children in the community and at school, and I have tried to connect with them, but only a few of them were interested in hearing these stories and being part of the community. I would always ask my fellow children about the community and the difference between a home and a community.

To my surprise, many of the children were not interested in the conversation because they wouldn't understand what I was talking about. Their parents only told them about their homes, not the community. Therefore, the children had no business to talk about the community. They were negative about the community. During this time, I got to understand that people love their homes, but they don't like the community. Today, I have noticed that many people spend time taking care of their homes and families and ignore the community. They don't discuss the community at home with the children. Based on this, some families don't even know their community. Therefore, they are not connecting with the community enough. I see this as a disconnection of leadership. If I distanced myself from the community that I live in, I would not only deprive myself of the community but also drive my children and the entire family away from the community. It's why my Dad's principles are critical in today's generation: learn and do not be the same, work with other people in mind, help others if you can, be willing to work and earn an income, and be a leader of your community. When you do, it will work for you and everybody around you.

Leadership that speaks for itself.

While perfection is not achievable in leadership, leadership decides perfection. Because leadership speaks for itself, this is what I experienced in my Dad's relationship with his four wives, living in the same home and raising their children without anger, divisiveness, hate, or fighting. I have only one wife, but I am struggling with it. How much more can I compare myself with one man who has four wives and who lives in the same home without a fight? It's about leadership roles and responsibility when you imagine my Dad's marital situation. It shows how leadership speaks for itself. It shows that my parents' behavior to hold onto their relationship to the final departure by death was superb.

Nothing of this can be compared to marriage relationships in the 21st century, In the 21st century, many people cannot keep their relationships even as they live apart in different cities. It's not because those people don't love each other, but it's because they lack leadership, set wrong goals, and are not humbled in the relationship. It's completely opposite to my parents' relationship. Apart from love, my parents showed leadership and set goals to live together, not to separate or divorce. They lived humbled in the relationship. Today, I believe my parents' achievement in such a long-term relationship was both individual and collective effort. My Dad and his four wives exercised leadership together. Individually, they took leadership roles and responsibility to the highest level of the relationship. They understand that being united means being together. Therefore, they planned and worked together, encouraged each other, and collectively led the family to a successful destination. As a result, there was no subpoena, no police intervention, no jail time, and no divorce.

How my Dad's illness became a story in my college years.

It was a long summer vacation in college, and I had just left for another state/region for a paid internship job to gain experience and make money to support myself at school. My parents had agreed with me to spend the summer vacation for the internship. However, the internship was not a formal internship where I could work in a well-structured company. It was a temporary summer contract, and I had to collaborate with different contractors to gain experience and make money for myself.

It was fun, and I enjoyed the work the entire time. However, one week after summer vacation was over and I was about to report to school, I was notified that my Dad was hospitalized and that it was serious. I took off at once and traveled to where my Dad lived. Upon arrival, my Dad had been discharged from the hospital a day ago and unfortunately went into a coma. Sadly, everybody had already given up on my Dad, saying that he was not going to survive the illness. According to my uncle, nobody had survived the sickness in the area before, and it was more proper to have my Dad passed away at home than in the hospital. I told my uncle that my Dad would rather pass away in the hospital than at home and at once took off with my Dad to the hospital. In the hospital, my Dad was admitted, and the medical staff put drips on him. In the first two days, my Dad regained enough consciousness, and after a week in the hospital, he was discharged home. Before he was discharged, his doctor recommended that he take his prescriptions accordingly and judiciously continue with physical therapy.

My Dad's recovery at home.

Because my Dad was recommended to take his prescriptions accordingly and continue with the physical therapy judiciously, I decided to stay with him at home to help him not only take the medications as prescribed but also with the physical therapy. My goal was to have my Dad walk on his feet before I could go back to school. Every day, I would put my arms around my Dad and walk him around the house two times a day. It took my Dad two weeks before he could hold a stick, stand on his feet, and begin moving his feet. While I was helping my Dad with this physical therapy, one month had already passed, and I had not returned back to school. This time, there was enough improvement, but I stayed a few days more to ensure that my Dad was comfortable walking around with his stick. While I care and worry about my Dad's health condition, he was also worried about me not going back to school. Over one month after school had resumed, my Dad called me into his room and said, "Go back to school. Do not let anything hold you back from your life journey. Do not let my sickness and the physical therapy hold you back from your life journey." I was shocked.

Here, my Dad was talking about leadership, role, and responsibility. As a parent, my Dad understands that he has a leadership role and responsibility to balance his needs with my needs while I take care of him. He also understands that, while I spend time with him trying to get him well and able to walk by himself again, I could be kicked out of school and lose my academic advancement. What he wants to put across here is that while you are holding back on something, you are losing out on something.

Holdback.

Holdback can be anything that holds you back or anything that you hold back from your leadership or person. It could be pride, selfego, anger, hate, divisiveness, or grudge. It could also be the pursuit of politics without leadership, role, and responsibility. Holdback is a misleading element that people don't critically look at in the big picture. Holdback constitutes most of the failures of leadership roles and responsibilities across the country. Many people find holdbacks as a new way of pursuing life. They embrace it as an entitlement. As a result, they mislead themselves and create chaos in society. Every day, holdback misleads people or politicians to pursue bad goals that affect the country.

Due to holdback, people don't want to change course. They want to stay on the wrong course and do the wrong things. Psychologically, holdbacks can prevent many people from bouncing back from wrong to right. Due to this, many people are overshadowed by their personal holdbacks or the holdbacks of their organization, community, or society that they are involved in. As a result, the holdback is clouding over society. It holds political leaders in bondage, citizens and noncitizens, immigrants and nonimmigrants from pursuing the values of the country, leadership, role, and responsibility. How do you understand your holdback? Your holdback hinders your leadership. If you do not understand your holdback, how would you enhance your leadership role and responsibility? You must know your holdback to balance it with leadership roles and responsibility. If you cannot name your holdback, then you are at the edge of directly or indirectly failing yourself and the society that you lead. This is why a holdback is an incredibly important element in you. When allowed, it can manifest in your actions. How do you know about your holdback? While you are holding back on something, you are losing out on something. Holdback can mislead you into thinking that your home is the same as your community, but it is not.

Home and community in the view of politics.

While you think your home is your community, your home is not your community. To achieve political goals, you must understand the difference between a home and a community. Your home is your political party, and your community is the country. When you lose your home, you can always live in the community. But when you lose your community, you have no home to live in. When you develop your mindset to uphold your home rather than the community, you have distanced yourself from the community. It means that by upholding your home, you are upholding the political party, not the country. Regardless of the potential for the party to form the government, you are still not connecting with your community enough. You don't get to collaborate with the community members. Eventually, your membership with the community will disconnect while you are still in leadership, leaving the community vulnerable to enemy attacks. This is where we are in the 21st century.

Many politicians are unable to differentiate between a home and community or a political party and country. This is a political holdback. Apolitical holdback could mislead a politician to undermine issues that matter to the country. Many politicians today are confused about their leadership role and responsibility in deciding what matters for the country. At the same time, others are also confused about what matters in the rule of law and the merit of fairness in society. Therefore, many politicians have mixed mindsets about matters of home and community. It's a political holdback. Political holdbacks have caused many people not to conduct their destined leadership roles and responsibilities in the best interest of the community and their homes. Political holdbacks disenfranchise national security and freedom.

holdbacks and national security and freedom.

While people are yet to discover the harm of political holdbacks in society, it's critical to know that dwelling on political holdbacks for leadership decisions hider national security and freedom. Anything that undermines national security also undermines the freedom of the people. It undermines the integrity of the country. For example, government shutdowns. Anytime a government shutdown is announced, the country goes into a panic while enemies abroad are jubilating for the failure of the government. When the government is subject to shutdown, the integrity of the leadership of the country is questioned. Shutting down the government is not political; it's personal. It goes beyond a political party. Because any decision to shut down the government affects the national security and freedom of the people and undermines the integrity of the country, it also affects the government's infrastructure. Therefore, shutting down the government is a political holdback. While political leaders often use a government shutdown as a political tool to expand political power, it's a political holdback. It undermines the leadership role and responsibility of the government.

Holdback as a leadership issue.

Holdback is a leadership issue. What are you holding back from your leadership? While holdback misleads, it can mislead you to make odd political decisions that can jeopardize your political goals and undermine the country. It can also mislead you to join a bad crowd and weaken your leadership potential to lead your people. Holdback is seen as a misleading element. When overshadowed by a holdback, you can undermine your leadership or the leadership of the country.

Your ambition to help your country sours when misled by a holdback. Holdback can cause you to flatten in politics, lose your leadership bond with your country, and weaken the leadership of your country abroad.

Holdback can cause you to narrow your mindset about leadership, roles, and responsibility to think that you can do anything in your leadership without sanctions. Holdback can again cause you to undermine the nation by focusing on a political party. Your party is your home, but your country is your community. Without your home, you can live in the community, but without your community, you have no home to live in. Regardless of your holdback, you are destined to lead your home and the community with honor. You are endorsed by the community into your position not only because you are destined for it but also because you are loved by it.

Therefore, making leadership decisions that affect the nation also affects the people. However, when you take your leadership personally, it becomes a holdback. In this way, your actions will not model the public. Your leadership role and responsibility are critical in your position not only because your actions will affect the public but also because of the legacy you leave behind. Do not take your leadership for granted, or else your actions will undermine the infrastructure of your community, wipe out the traditional values of your country, and create a new America. There is not a single person exempted from a holdback, but when you overcome it, you will not only affect your family and community, but also you will positively affect the entire society.

Holdback and parenting.

While parenting is the act of parents nurturing the kids from birth to legal adulthood, some parents are the reason why a holdback is born and grows in a child. A child is not born to be divisive, hate people, or be politically angry with people. A child is born unique and must grow unique. It is the duty of the parent to shape a child's life. This duty is an obligation that was ordered by God. Therefore, it is critical to know that parents are destined to nurture a child positively and right. Parents have leadership roles and responsibilities to help their children grow into productive adult citizens. This privilege of parents is often taken for granted. Parents often trade their obligation to positively nurture kids with their personal holdbacks. During parenting, parents will talk negatively about people in the community instead of modeling the kids with a positive mindset. Mostly self-petit stuff that will dialogue negatively in the child and cause the child a lot more harm than good to think that what they hear their parents talk about was the right choice of endeavor. Often, kids are susceptive to information. In other words, kids receive information as parents tell them. If parents see a child as a unique person in society, they will manage their holdbacks within themselves to avoid transferring their holdbacks to the child. Once you transfer your holdback to the child, it will follow the child to the leadership. According to the scripture, a good person will not give a child a stone when the child asks for bread (Matthew 7:9-12). Regardless of your holdback, you cannot give your child a stone when they ask for bread. This principle is critical in leadership, role, and responsibility.

Holdback and fail leadership.

Your failure in leadership will not come from who you are or what you do but from what you hold back. Congress enacts laws, a police officer enforces the law, A judge decides on cases, or a teacher teaches. When the Congressman or woman, the police officer, the judge, or the teacher takes their duty to the highest level of leadership, they will have zero failures as the outcome because each post has principles to follow. When you follow the principles, you are going to achieve a positive result. However, when you walk out of the principles and pursue your holdback, you are subject to failure. Because you are not practicing what you are trained for in the position. You cannot be negative and expect to lead positively. You can figure this argument out mathematically.

In Mathematics, when you multiply negative five by positive five, it gives you negative ten. Also, when you add negative ten to positive ten, the results will be zero. Either way, you have not achieved anything negative while pretending to be positive. It is how a holdback is manifested in you and your leadership. One thing to care about is that a holdback is a misleading element. It can mislead you at any time if you do not uphold your leadership role and responsibility to the highest level of your duty. Therefore, being a congressman or woman, police officer, judge, teacher, or the President of the United States, your failure in leadership will not come from who you are or what you are doing but from what you hold back.

Holdback in the Congress.

The divisiveness, anger, and hate in the Congress today is not political. It is a holdback. The pattern of anger and divisiveness in Congress shows that Congressmen and women are overshadowed by personal and collective holdbacks. Because divisiveness, anger, and hate in Congress are happening even within individual political parties. It's something to worry about the Congress. It's usual to have different political views in the same party, but it's not usual to have divisiveness, anger, and hate in the same political party.

So, when the Congressmen and women see themselves as one body, they work as a united Congress. They will model each other and engage in politics and policies that are right for the country, fair and just. They will also maintain the country's traditional entitlement, including leadership, role, and responsibility. However, when Congressmen and women decide to work in divisive ways in their own party and across other political parties, they do not work for the interests of the country. They work for self-interest. This is a holdback. Holdback misleads and can mislead you at any time if it depends on yourself.

While you allow your personal holdback to overshadow your politics and policies, you are breaking your leadership bond with your country or weakening the country's leadership abroad. While you can downplay your home improvements, you cannot downplay the improvements of your community. Because your community is paramount, it is critical to know that your country is your community, but your party is your home. When you lose your home, you can always live in the community, but when you lose your community, you lose your home. Expand your experience in politics and policies, yet walk out of holdbacks because it can cause you to mislead people in leadership.

Holdback and gun control

While the government believes that banning an assault weapon will end gun violence, I believe it is a holdback. Is there any weapon that does not kill? Why should one weapon be targeted as an assault when every weapon kills? To me, banning assault weapons in the United States simply means banning all weapons in the country. It is the act of disarming the country. This is a holdback. One thing that the government did not acknowledge is that every gun incident across the country involves only one gunman, killing many people. If every one of those people killed had a gun with them, they would never have been killed. Due to people's lack of guns with them, many people are killed.

My Dad used to say that if you cannot help me resolve my case, do not make matters worse for me. What I want to put across here is that if the government cannot supply a weapon to every household or individual that is screened and well to own a gun, it should not disarm the public. When you disarm society, you have disabled the people. It is a holdback. Arm people when they are qualified to own a gun. It helps people protect themselves when they're in danger of getting killed by a gunman. Two of the several ways to end gun violence in the United States are (1) invest in mental health awareness and management, (2) invest in state gun screening centers to issue identifications for buying guns, and (3) encourage security and surveillance systems at homes and organizations to track people with the potential to commit a crime.

Mental health management

Ignoring the reality of increasing mental health issues across the country puts the mentally sick population at risk of harm. It is a holdback. Without research, it is apparent that after the COVID-19 pandemic, many people are left with mental health challenges: anxiety, depression, loneliness, divorce, and/or people mourning for their loved ones who perished during COVID-19. Knowingly or unknowingly, the government sees mental health issues as less critical while campaigning to ban assault weapons. Due to this, the government has taken its focus from investing in mental health screening and management. However, the government is critical of Congress hoping to pass a law that will ban AR-15s from the market. This is a holdback.

While the government is wasting time investing in mental health, the mentally sick population that is quick to commit a crime with a gun increases. This poses a potential risk of gun violence in society. This holdback of the government does not only deprive the mentally health population from getting financial support for screening and managing their mental issues, but it also increases the chance of mass killings in society. Mentally sick populations are vulnerable without financial resources to manage their symptoms. Their vulnerability will only increase their mental health issues, leaving them with evil options. The option is to look for a gun and kill innocent people. Based on this, people kill people. Guns don't kill people. This is what I see happening in American society. What are you holding back in your leadership?

Holdback and Insurrection

If you believe that the January 6 insurrection was purposeful, I do not. It was not purposeful. It was a holdback. Even though I came to understand that it was a well-planned event, it was still not purposeful. It was a holdback. The holdback manifested into small talks and eventually resulted in what you saw as insurrection. Every holdback calls for small talk. Small talks about holdbacks are always misleading. Because the conversation about holdbacks often stimulates the mind and causes you to perceive your holdback as a genuine endeavor. When this happens, there is no bullet to stop you from acting it out. Because you will be excited, motivated, and determined to pursue the course. It is what I believe happened. What about you? If you saw it differently, what would it be? Holdback is a misleading element. When overshadowed, it can mislead you to an unintended action. This is what I experienced during the January 6 insurrection. Everybody who took part in the January 6 insurrection did not mean to have it happen the way it did to the country. But they were all misled by the holdback. Actions due to holdbacks have a pattern.

Holdback and government

To analyze the role of a holdback in government, it's fair to examine what I experienced in four years of President Trump's government. Over the period of President Trump's government, many people were fired, resigned, prosecuted, or went to jail. This was a holdback. People should not be fired, resign, prosecuted, or go to jail in the course of serving the government in the United States. But when it happens, it triggers a red flag about the leadership role and responsibility of the government. While nobody knows about what really happened in President Trump's cabinet, you could tell that the government underwent a circle of leadership, role, and responsibility issues. You could also tell that the government could not balance the holdback with the leadership role and responsibility. As a result, many people were fired, resigned, prosecuted, or went to jail. However, holdbacks in governments are common. But every successful government welcomes all voices in the cabinet. They welcome all democratic voices, including conservative, progressive, liberal, or independent voices. All these voices play a role in achieving the goals of the government. However, the government must strategize its policies to balance holdbacks across the board and allow the government to efficiently function for the country.

Holdback and George Floyd's death.

What happened between the Minneapolis police officer and George Floyd was a holdback. The police officer was overshadowed by a holdback to end George Floyd's life. It was not what the officer intended to do for the day, but it was what he did for the day. It was a holdback. It is how a holdback is manifested in an officer on duty. I will bet with you that this officer was dispatched many times in his police career and did an excellent job. However, on this bright, sunny day in Minneapolis, this officer was dispatched to respond to a judgment call in the community. This time it was George Floyd. As usual, he went through his checklist and apprehended George Floyd to keep law and order. The next from the checklist was to transport George Floyd to the jail, but the officer was overshadowed by a holdback. Therefore, he turned George Floyd down and sat on his neck until George Floyd passed out. Whether this was a coincidence or an accident, it was a holdback.

George Floyd is gone and will not come back to life. The officer is still in jail with a red jumpsuit. I don't think this was the legacy that the officer had signed for when he was hired. But it is the legacy that he met. It could happen to anybody in many ways. It is the result of a holdback. In this case, the holdback was the officer's behavior, which caused him to act beyond the official duty of his career. Behavior that kicked up after he apprehended George Floyd had George Floyd killed. What I want to put across here is that your holdback can mislead you to lose sight of your positive leadership, role, and responsibility and pursue the negative goals that can lead you to negative actions and negative consequences. Watch your actions. It could be a holdback.

My last encounter with my Dad.

My last encounter with my Dad in 2015 changed the entire spectrum of my worldview. It was an awakening moment. It was a moment that I felt my trip to my Dad was well accomplished. It was a moment of knowledge. A moment when I learned to understand the significance of leadership, role, and responsibility. It all happened when my Dad was sick and asked that I pay him a visit to his home in a small town in the Upper East Region, Ghana. My Dad had requested several times that I should visit him. It was usually based on my relationship with my Dad. However, it was an exceedingly challenging time for me and my family because I was going through marital issues.

My relationship soured, and I did not want to reveal it to my Dad at that time. I had thought that it would be heartbreaking to meet my Dad for the first time in seventeen years with marital issues while he was sick. These holdbacks were enough for me to put off my Dad's calls. However, while I was putting off my Dad's calls, he kept on sending messages to me. At that time, I would go to bed and could not sleep on time. I began missing my Dad every day and night while feeling guilty for not connecting with him enough. It was an ambiguous situation. I entered prayers, looking for God's guidance to do the right thing. At that time, I received a revelation in a small voice, "Songtiib, how long would you continue hiding your marital situation from your Dad?" This was it! I regained myself and said oh, I must go to my Dad and fulfill my Dad's calls. At this time, I bought a plane ticket and flew to my Dad and listened to him.

My trip to my Dad in Ghana in 2015.

My trip to my Dad was successful. I arrived at my Dad's residence safely. It was at night, and my Dad was fast asleep. I did attempt to wake my Dad up, but I remembered what he used to tell me when I was growing up, "Don't wake me up in sleep unless in an emergency situation; any last chance I get to sleep is very important to me." Due to this, I obeyed my Dad's word and did not wake him up in the middle of the night.

Due to my eagerness to meet with my Dad, I could not sleep that night. However, my Dad used to ask me for some outfits which I brought with me. I intentionally placed the outfit on his chair so that when he woke up in the morning, he would know that I was home.

That night, my Dad woke up earlier than usual, found the outfit on his chair, and screamed, "Songtiib is here." I overheard him from my room, and I opened my door and rushed to him, and we hugged each other. I tore down and sat on the bench beside him, and we talked for about two hours before everybody woke up. My Dad and I had a long, cordial conversation. After this, I spent one week with my Dad. However, every day was a new day for me and my Dad. We would sit under a neem tree in front of the house and talk about the past and present. My Dad was happy for my wife and children.

He asked me if I had a good relationship with my family. I told my Dad how much I love my family. During this weeklong conversation, I asked my Dad this question: "Do you think I should marry more than one wife?" I know my Dad had married four wives and they still live together with him. My Dad said, "Do what matters for your society." This is it. I was thrilled. I could not believe what my Dad just said! My Dad did not say I should do what I need or what I want, but he said I should do what matters for my society. Here, my Dad was talking about leadership, role, and responsibility. If I did what matters to my society, then I would have a duty. I have a duty not to do what I need and what I want but to do what matters to my society.

Do what matters to your society.

If I would do what matters for my society or my generation, I would hold onto what I do for myself, my family, and my community. My Dad did not tell me to do what I needed for my society or what I wanted for my society, but he said I should do what matters for my society. With this obligation, I was able to develop innovative approaches to reconnect with my spouse, enhance my communication with her, and manage the family in a way that was healthy for the family. It was not what I needed or what I wanted, but what mattered for the family. It's the heart of leadership, roles, and responsibility. As a parent, I understand that I have a duty to do what matters to my family and community. I understand that I must balance my wants and needs with what matters to my family.

As time went on, I learned and understood that the challenges I face every day are challenges to meet my needs and wants. However, I understand that if I could do what matters for myself every day, I would not worry about my needs and wants. Because it will balance out, it means that if I keep on doing what matters every day, I will not only balance the needs and wants of myself but also the needs and wants of my family. Based on this, it is critical to examine what you are doing, whether it matters for the business, your society, or both. Now, are you doing what matters for your society? As a parent, manager, Congressman, woman, governor, or the President of the United States, are you doing what matters for your society, or are you doing what you need or want? While you think about doing what matters for your society, are you doing what matters for your companionships around you?

Achieving the best of companionships

To achieve the best in your companionship, you must do what matters for the relationship. My Dad said to me, "Do what matters for your society." He did not tell me to do what I like, what I need, or what I want, but he said I should do what matters for my society. Are you doing what matters for your society? Society is large, but everybody has some form of relationship in this society. However, you are associated with society; whether you are fellowshipping with a family, business, religion, or politics, you have companionship with society. To achieve the best of these companionships, you have a leadership role and responsibility to do what matters for your companionships.

You are not doing what you need, what you like, or what you want for the relationship, but you are doing what matters. Regardless of your position, it is critical to know and understand that there is no end to what you like, what you need, or what you want in your relationships with society, whether family, business, or politics. How many times have you spent pursuing your needs or wants in your companionships, yet you haven't achieved them? What is achievable is what matters. The best way to achieve your relationships or companionships is to do what matters. Are you doing what matters in your companionships with yourself, family, neighbors, coworkers, or your business and/or employees? While you are sacrificing your time to do what matters for your companionship, it is critical to understand the nature of relationships.

Understand the nature of relationships.

Once the relationship is set up and going, every one of you has a leadership role and responsibility to do what matters in the relationship. This is the only best way you can manage your companionship's wants and needs to the best of your ability. It makes a lot of difference when you focus on doing what matters in the relationship rather than pursuing what you like, what you want, and/or what you need in the relationship. When you take a husband and wife, for instance, there is no way both can agree on everything before it happens. However, both can agree to do whatever matters for the relationship, whether collectively or individually.

In this way the couples can discuss their weaknesses freely and create room for advancing the relationship. Regardless, it is not a reality to be happy every day in your relationship, but it is a reality to do what matters for the relationship every day. It is how you can collectively or individually pursue your leadership role and responsibility in the relationship. Take a note! Your daily needs and wants are different from those of your spouse. Understanding this is all you need to enhance your relationship. You can set up your plans to go to Hawaii next week, but your spouse's can be the opposite. Your spouse might want to go to Washington, DC. This fat check is telling you that you could have a conflict trying to convince your spouse. If your spouse doesn't want to go to Hawaii, you don't get to go to Hawaii. If you aim to achieve that goal, you can lose your spouse. Often, ask yourself quick questions if it really matters for you to go to Hawaii. However, when you decide to head to Hawaii based on your needs and allow your spouse to go to Washington, DC, you are going to miss the target of your relationship. You are not going to curve the relationship. Because you are pursuing your needs and wants, based on this, it is critical to understand the nature of relationships or companionship when you are navigating through your relationships with your family and neighbors in the community.

Neighbors and community

Your family, neighbor, and community are three of the best companionships to have in your person. The things that matter in your relationship with your spouse also matter in your companionship with your neighbors and community. The most durable companionship is your family, your neighbor, and your community. To understand your neighbor is the first step in understanding your community. If you do not have any relationship with your neighbor, you don't have any relationship with your community. You and your neighbor are in one segment of the community. Your companionship with your neighbor makes your relationship with the community healthy. If you confide in your work and home, you do not get to socialize with your community. It means that you do not connect with the community enough. However, when you are asked about how you are doing in the community, you are most likely to say that you are doing well. However, you are not doing well because you do not partner with the community. To keep a healthy community, everybody's leadership role and responsibility is needed. It's critical to know that a healthy community produces a healthy family and youth. The youth are often influenced by the culture of the community. Therefore, your relationship in the community matters not only for your family but also for your neighbors and the youth. Regardless of your daily routine, try to connect with the community in whichever way fits your temperament, including through donations or financial support. Enhancing community relationships is not about what you need or what you want but whatever matters to the community. If you can achieve this, you can help make your workers and work environment welcoming.

Work and workers

Your effort in doing what matters in your relationship with your neighbors and community does not end up in the community, but it follows you to your work environment, where you partner with your staff, coworkers, or bosses. Your companionship with your staff, coworkers, and bosses is healthy if every one of you does what matters for the business. Thus, work in teams, build business relationships where you can trust each other, and communicate the business to the highest level of your leadership. Without better business relationships, people will hustle to get work done every day. There will be no better outcomes for business without better collaboration.

Most often, I asked myself, how would life look like in the work environment if everybody did what they liked, what they needed, or what they wanted? Probably, work will not be done. They would party at work, drink, and forget about work. However, people go to work and do what matters for the business. How do you do in your work environment? How do you associate with everybody at work? As a manager, what kind of relationship do you have with your staff?

How do you reach out to them every day? As a staff member, how do you collaborate with your supervisors and coworkers? Is everybody doing what matters for the business? The best relationships that matter for the work environment are that everybody understands the nature of the business, works as a team, collaborates on ideas, and helps each other however possible.

Business and employees

To achieve the best relationships in your business with your employees and clients, do not take your business into your own hands. Empower employees to take leadership of the business and help move the business forward. Employees value the companionship of the business when they understand the business. They value the business not only because of the paycheck but also because they love the business and what the business is advocating for society. Every employee who applies for a job in your business likes the company. When the employees secure their jobs and develop an attachment to the business, they need your leadership to grow in the business. Your leadership role and responsibility are critical to meeting your staff halfway in the effort. Most often, employees not only need training in the business but also guidance/coaching to help them integrate into the culture of the business and perform efficient jobs. In this way, you are not only doing what you need or want but also what matters for the employees and the business. It is the heart of leadership, role, and responsibility. It helps you achieve your companionship with your employees and business and move the business to the next level of your dream.